Resting Place: Déjà Vu

Resting Place Series Book Three

Resting Place: Déjà Vu
Resting Place Series Book Three

Mary M Beasley

LewMar Innovations, LLC
Silver Spring, MD

Copyright© 2019 Mary M Beasley

All rights reserved. No part of this book may be used or reproduced by any means, graphic, electronic, or mechanical, including photocopying, recording, taping, or by any information storage retrieval system without the written permission of the publisher except, in the case of brief quotations embodied in critical articles and reviews.

Any people depicted in stock imagery provided by Fiverr Designs are models, and such images are being used for illustrative purposes only. Certain stock imagery © Fiverr Designs.

Scriptures taken from the New King James Version, Copyright 1979, 1980, 1982 by Thomas Nelson, Inc. Used by permission. All rights reserved.

Editors:
Christine Wilson, Scrib4Him
Pirkko O'Clock

ISBN: 978-0-9986604-3-1

Printed in the United States of America.

For nothing is secret
that will not be revealed,
nor anything hidden that
will not be known and
come to light.
Luke 8:17

Dedications

This book is dedicated to my Heavenly Father, my Lord and Savior, Jesus Christ, and Holy Spirit. Thank you for giving me a love for words and the ability to create! I am so grateful.

To Lewis, my husband and best friend, the one who walks with me through all seasons. Thank you for our journey! 1-4-3

To my children, Cody, Amber, Amir, Marcus, Britmarie, and Lewis, you guys are my treasures!

To Chris, I am beyond grateful to have you in my life. Thank you for sharing your gifts with me.

To Pirkko, once again, you have blessed me with your refiner's pen and caused my word to flow.

Prologue

Hector was enraged. She wouldn't wake up! How could he have his revenge when Monica was sound asleep? He had slapped her around but couldn't wake her. Little Joe must have given her too much stuff. He didn't have time to wait until the stuff wore off. He would just have to kill her, put a bullet in her head. He hated this; he had waited years to kill her slowly, to punish her for betraying him, but now all he would get was to shoot her. Hector slapped her again, "Come on, Monica; wake up!"

Hector and Little Joe stood over the woman in the corner of the room, unaware of the shadow that eased through the door, and stood behind Little Joe. Hector heard a grunt; then, Little Joe hit the floor hard. He shone his light in that direction but saw nothing. "Who's there?" Hector said in a strained voice. "Who's there?" Hector looked around again and then pointed his gun at the woman's head.

Trace and Lilly were in the shack's closet; they heard the man fall to the floor and the fear in Hector's voice. Trace pointed his gun, ready to take a shot. "Trace, no. He might shoot her. Let me distract him." Lilly whispered.

Trace whispered, "Okay."

Lilly mustered her courage and said, "Hector, for a drug lord, you sure are stupid. You couldn't even kidnap the right woman."

"Monica? Monica! Where are you? Show yourself, or I'll kill her." Shining his light around the room, Hector couldn't see anyone.

Trace threw his keys across the room. Hector shot towards the keys. Then Trace took his shot, hitting Hector in his right leg. Hector grunted with pain and then grabbed the woman on the floor. "I'll kill her! I'll kill her!" Hector yelled while backing toward the door.

Trace saw a man appear behind Hector when he reached the door. Hector shoved the woman towards the direction where he had heard Monica's voice. As Hector turned to run, the man behind him delivered a punch to his jaw that dropped him to the floor. He was out cold. Trace shone his light on the man, "Sam, what are you doing here?"

Sam smiled and said, "Ben asked me to hang around just in case he needed an extra pair of hands. Hey, you got some cuffs on you? The one over there is going to be out for a while," Sam said, pointing at Little Joe. "I found the chloroform he used on that little lady and decided to give him a taste of his own medicine. This other one should be coming around in a few minutes, and I want to make sure he doesn't get away."

Trace pulled out his cuffs and handed them to Sam, then called Ben, letting him know they had found Maria. She was unconscious but alive, and they needed to get her to the hospital as soon as possible. They also needed some backup for Hector and his man. Trace could hear the faint sounds of the ambulance in the distance as he put away his cell phone.

Chapter One

Tate Weston's heart was pounding as he rushed from the parking lot into Resting Place Hospital. Maria was awake! After three torturous days of watching her in a coma, he needed to see her, talk with her, and make sure she was okay.

Clinically she was stable, with no broken bones, no major head injury, outside of the bruises on her face and arms. Her Neurologist, Dr. Bryan Hinton, a colleague, and a friend, informed Tate that clinically, there was no reason why she was in a coma. The testing showed normal brain function; she just appeared to be sleeping.

Currently existing on a couple of hours of sleep, after completing his second shift in the ER, Tate's habit for the past three days had been to make his way to Maria's room and talk with her about his day, pray for her, and then fall asleep in the chair next to her bed. Then, in the wee hours of the morning, he would head home before the morning shift started.

Tate realized that his colleagues, friends, and family noticed that his behavior had changed. He was acting out of character. Maria wasn't his patient, so why was he spending so much time with her? Uncle Ben suspected something was going on but didn't say anything, and Tate couldn't bring himself to talk with anyone about Maria. The feelings he had for her were too new. It was crazy how much he cared for her. He had only spent one day with her. One incredibly mind-blowing day that had changed his life. He didn't know how to begin to explain his relationship to anyone. All he knew was they had connected, and they both were aware that what they shared was special.

Caught off-balance, from the moment Tate met Officer Maria Rodriguez, she was like no other woman he had ever known. Maria was so direct, straightforward; her honesty caught him off guard, causing him to respond before he could think about what to say. He never spoke without thinking; that changed when he met Maria.

≈≈≈

While Tate and Maria worked together that day, their conversation was casual, but the air around them hummed with an electrical charge that they couldn't ignore. Later that morning, Tate was so baffled about his feelings and so deep in thought about why he felt so much with this woman that he developed a constant frown trying to figure it out.

Maria watched Tate frown at her for most of that morning, she decided to ignore him, but as frustration turned to anger, she blurted out, "Dr. Weston, why are you frowning at me?"

Tate heard the sharpness in her voice but also saw the pain that she was unable to hide. "I'm sorry, it's not you. Please forgive me for making you feel uncomfortable." He tried to smile, but that frown reappeared.

That must have been the last straw for her; Maria went off! Speaking fast in Spanish and English, her honey-brown eyes were ablaze with fire. Tate couldn't help it; he just stared at her; she was stunning. He usually didn't like making a scene or drama of any kind, but this woman fascinated him. Then the frown was back again, as he realized at that very moment he was falling; never had Tate felt what he was feeling about a woman.

"Maria. Maria. Maria!"

Maria fell silent, but the look in her eyes was still screaming at him in two different languages.

Tate walked over to her with an apologetic smile, "I'm sorry, I know this looks bad, but I can explain."

Putting her hands on her hips, Maria stared and demanded, "What?" She waited impatiently for an explanation. She was ready to read him the riot act if he even hinted at her not being competent for this assignment.

Tate was so surprised that he said the first thing that came to his mind. "I'm attracted to you." Seeing the stunned look on her face, he tried to verbalize what he had been trying to process all morning. "There is this chemistry, this energy between us, and I've never experienced it before, and I'm not sure what to do about it."

Maria couldn't believe what she was hearing. This man was actually telling her that he is attracted to her, and he had never felt this way about anyone. She couldn't believe that just this morning, she had caught her now ex-boyfriend, Jesse, cheating on her. For a while, she had suspected him because he'd made several excuses and stood her up on more than one occasion. She had used her vacation time with her family to evaluate her relationship and had decided that she would talk to him about going their separate ways. That conversation wasn't necessary when she stopped by his apartment on her way to Resting Place and found that Jesse was not alone and that his lady friend made sure that Maria knew it. Maria got the message and walked away without saying a word. It was over, and to her surprise, it didn't hurt. Jesse never generated any sparks in her. She really didn't know why she hadn't ended the relationship sooner.

Now this man, Dr. Tate Weston, had her wondering if her hair was standing on ends with the electricity he produced. It was almost funny; then she laughed. The release from all the day's events felt great. Maria had struggled all morning with the attraction she had for Tate; it was a relief to know that she was not the only one struggling. Tate was honest about his feelings and direct with her. She liked him, and she felt comfortable with him, and all of a sudden, she wanted to learn more about Dr. Tate Weston.

Tate watched Maria as her face change from shock to thoughtful; then, he heard the most incredible sound he had ever heard, her laughter. Then he frowned again, wondering if she was laughing at him.

"Dr. Weston," Maria said, wiping tears from her eyes, "If you can frown because you are attracted to me, why can't I laugh if I'm attracted to you?" Her question hung in the air as Tate processed what she just said, then they both burst out laughing, releasing the pent-up tension until tears came, and they were out of breath.

After laughing and lots of smiling, Tate reached for her hand. Maria looked at his long, lean fingers as she put her hand in his, wondering why it was so easy to take his hand. It took months before she allowed Jesse to hold her hand, and she didn't like how it felt. Tate walked her over to a loveseat, sat down, and began talking in low voices; they seemed to have developed an urgent desire to know one another.

Tate and Maria shared their likes, dislikes, hopes, and dreams. They talked about their cars, her mustang, some of the old cars Tate had restored, and his Oldsmobile 442. Then out of the blue, Maria asked, "Tell me a secret, something you haven't told anybody before."

Chapter Two

Tell her a secret… Tate looked at her, captivated by her and intrigued by the prospect of sharing with anyone on such a personal level, then responded, "I will tell you a secret if you will share a secret with me." He stood up and reached for her hands, and lifted her into his arms. Pulling her into his arms was as natural as breathing air to him. He wondered if holding her would always feel so good, so right, and at that moment, he knew. He knew that this incredible fireball was the one for him.

Standing together face to face looking into each other's eyes, Maria shared, "I'm not supposed to know this, and my parents don't know that I know that my Dad is not my biological father. I overheard them talking one night when they thought I was asleep. Before they got married, my Mom was attacked and raped. My Dad told my mom that night that I was his daughter, his child, and no matter how many children they have, I would always be their firstborn, and no one would ever take me away from him. I remember my Mom crying and them kissing that night before I went to bed."

Tate tighten his hold on her in a warm embrace before asking, "How do you feel about that?"

She pulled back and said, "I love my dad, and I know he loves me. I have three brothers, Rafel, Carlos, and Anthony; he loves us all the same. I have never told anyone, not even my parents, that I know this."

Tate stared into her honey-brown eyes and responded, "I am honored to share that secret with you, and I promise you, it is safe with me." Tate's gaze dropped to her lips, and she reached up to kiss him. As he closed his eyes, he couldn't capture all the emotions affecting him. All he could do was feel them. Tate had never felt so out of control, and yet it felt like his whole life had just aligned. It felt right.

Pulling back both of them, a little breathless, Tate said, "Wow."

Smiling, Maria whispered, "Wow." Then, clearing her throat, she said, "Your turn."

Tate took a half step back, capturing her eyes again before saying, "When I was 15 years old, I made God a promise that I would honor Him and my future wife with my body by remaining celibate until my wedding night."

Maria just stared. After a prolonged tension-filled pause, she asked, "Have you kept that promise?"

Tate moved closer, "Yes, I have. I also told God that I'd only share that information with the one I intended sharing my life with." Then he lowered his head again, claiming her lips.

Tate's ringing phone caused them to pull apart; Maria took several steps away from him. She couldn't think, could barely see straight. Wow, no man had ever affected her this way. Did he say something about sharing his life with her? The attraction they shared was crazy; she had just met him. Why did it feel so right? How can I trust him so completely? Why was she entertaining a future with Dr. Tate Weston?

When Tate hung up the phone, he looked at her and asked, "Are you okay?" He smiled, and it melted something deep inside, calming her with one smile.

"Yes, I'm okay, Tate, this is a lot…."

"I know it is, but I want to see where we go from here, Maria. I have never felt like I do right now, and I believe it is God. Maria, can we slow down a little bit and see what God has for us? When this case is over, can I see you?"

"Yes, Tate, I would like that."

Tate gave her a brilliant smile and a quick kiss and said, "Ben needs me downstairs. Brandy will be up in a couple of minutes. But first, I want a picture with you." Taking out his phone, he put his left arm around Marie and snapped a picture. They exchanged phone numbers, and Tate texted her a copy of the photo with the scripture, 'Proverbs 18:22', after another quick kiss, Brandy entered the room, and Tate left.

Smiling, Maria recalled the scripture, *He who finds a wife finds a good thing And obtains favor from the Lord.* Maria took a deep breath and tried to think logically; before today, romance, relationships, and marriage were definitely not on her shortlist of priorities. Meeting Tate changed everything. In just one day, she was thinking about all three, and amazingly, she was looking forward to seeing what God had in store for her and Tate Weston.

Maria's mom had told her many times when she complained about adjusting her life to please a man. Then, Rosa Rodrigue would smile and say, "Baby girl, when you fall in love, it will be like nothing you have ever felt before, and you will be more than willing to make adjustments in your schedule and your life. It will be easy; that's when you will know that it's real love." Maria smiled again; she couldn't wait to tell her Mama about Tate.

Breaking glass caused her to spin around and reach for her gun. Before she could aim it, a huge man in all black rushed her with a white towel in his hand, shoving it in her face. Pushing his hand away, she could smell the sweet odor from the towel that turned rotten. Then, shaking her head, trying to clear it, she heard Brandy telling her to run, but Brandy's voice was fading, sounding far away. Door —got—to run. Maria could feel herself falling; her last thought was that Tate would come, then blackness.

Chapter Three

Tate rushed into the hospital room, smiling, "Maria! Thank God you're awake!" Unable to contain the joy he was feeling. Tate leaned over and gently pull her into his arms, "I am so glad you're awake. I wanted to come when you went missing, but Kevin was wounded, and I had to stop the bleeding…."

"Dr. Weston!" Startled, Tate turned to find an older couple, the woman seated looked like an older version of Maria, and the man, standing with murder in his eyes, had to be her dad.

"Chief and Mrs. Rodriguez. I'm sorry I didn't notice you when I came in." Tate was thankful for his caramel coloring, which hid some of the blush heating his face.

"Obviously. Why are you groping my daughter?"

Tate heard the quiet warning in his voice, making him feel like a kid caught kissing after a date.

Then, Maria's mom spoke up, "Tony, maybe it would be good to talk with Dr. Weston outside?" She was the same height as Maria, but the look she gave Chief Rodriguez demonstrated where Maria got her fire. Tate smiled, remembering when that same look was directed at him. Then, with a nod of his head, the Chief led the way out of the room.

Rosa Rodriguez had watched as the young doctor hurried into the room, paused, stared, and then gently gathered her daughter in his arms, whispering in her ear. He was holding her as if she was the finest of treasures. First, she saw the blank look on Maria's face; then, when he hugged her, a smile of contentment crossed her face that Rosa had never seen on Maria. Of course, Rosa knew that look, but how? How could her cautious, standoffish daughter feel safe in this stranger's arms?

"Mom? What's going on? Who was that man?" Maria asked with a slight frown, rubbing her temples.

"Maria, honey, are you in pain? Should I get the nurse?"

"No, Mama, I'm okay. I'm sure I look a lot worst than I feel. My doctor told me I took quite a beating, but I don't remember anything about it. I guess that's a good thing."

"Yes, you have a lot of bruises, but they will fade, and you will be as good as new." Rosa said, blinking back tears, clearing her throat, she continued, "The man who was hugging you is Dr. Tate Weston. Do you know him?"

"No, I don't know him."

"Are you sure? He acted like you were friends, more than friends."

Maria shook her head, evoking pain, causing her to rub her temples again, "Ma, if I had met Dr. Tate Weston, even in passing, I would remember it."

"Maybe, maybe not, your doctor said, you seem to be experiencing some short-term memory loss. You could have met him while on this last assignment. It's possible, yes?"

Maria laughed, "Mama, the possibility of us meeting and becoming friends or more than friends is so incredibly unlikely. He's a doctor, we move in different social circles, and besides, that's not who I am. You know how long it took for me to go out with Jesse, and we still haven't progressed to the level of kissing. It's just not who I am."

Rosa gave her a small smile that Maria recognized she used when she knew something nobody else knew. Then said, "So why did you let him hold you, and from where I sat, you looked like you enjoyed the attention."

Maria's honey brown cheeks turned a becoming rose color as she cleared her throat and responded, "I don't know, it felt, I felt safe, I can't explain it, but I felt safe."

≈≈≈

Tate walked behind Chief Rodriguez, trying to think how he could explain his relationship with Maria, and bumped into Chief Rodriguez as he turned around, demanding, "Dr. Weston, what were you doing with my daughter?"

"Chief Rodriguez, with all due respect, if you want to know about my relationship with Maria, you need to talk with her." No way was he going to talk with her dad without talking to Maria.

"I would if I could." Chief Rodriguez let out a frustrated breath. "I don't know you, all I know is I sent my baby girl on assignment with Ben Rayns, and now she's beat up and doesn't remember anything from the last few days."

Tate listened, his stomach dropping as if he experienced a sudden nosedive as understanding dawned on him. He asked, "She doesn't remember? Anything?"

"The last thing she remembers is eating breakfast with us, then leaving for that assignment. Ben couldn't share anything about the case, and I get that, but I know that you were with her. Can you tell me anything?"

Tate watched Maria's father relay the information with slumped shoulders and realized that this man felt as helpless as Tate did. Hearing her father's words and remembering the secret Maria shared with him caused Tate to rethink and tell him about the time they shared. Somehow Tate knew he would understand. "Sir, I can't share what I know about the case, but I can talk about the time I spent with Maria. The friendship we share."

"Thank you; I would appreciate that." Tate talked for about forty-five minutes, leaving out the secrets and the kisses they shared. He even confessed to slipping into her hospital room, spending most of his nights watching over her, telling her about his day.

As he finished talking, Chief Rodriguez looked him in the eyes and asked, "So what are you saying, Dr. Weston?"

Tate straightened in his chair and responded, "Sir, I know we haven't known each other for very long, but we both knew that what we experienced, the connection we shared, was special. Maria agreed to see me after the case was over." Taking a deep breath, Tate continued, "Sir, with your permission, I would like to court your daughter."

"You do know; she is already in a relationship, don't you?"

"She may not remember, but she visited him before coming to Resting Place and found that he was not alone. So she ended that relationship before we met."

"She shared a lot with you." It wasn't a question, more like acknowledging a fact. The comment stirred something in Tate.

"It was the best day of my life."

"You know she doesn't remember any of this? The doctor says her memory may or may not come back and advised us not to force it. Let it come back naturally. Are you willing to pursue her, to win her affection again?"

"Sir, I have no choice."

Smiling, Chief Rodriguez extended his hand and said, "Since you're going to be around, I guess you better call me Tony."

"Thank you, sir, uh Tony."

Chapter Four

Jesse Mendez sat in his leather lazy boy chair, staring aimlessly around his luxurious living room, sipping his coffee, thinking about the events of the last few days. Everything was on schedule. His lady friend in Personnel had told him that his promotion paperwork was submitted. He was so happy he wanted to celebrate, so he invited her out to dinner. After a satisfying meal, he invited her in for a satisfying night. He had given her some extra attention quenching his long-starved hunger from being put off by Maria Rodriguez. How could he woo this one with all her high morals? She barely let him hold her hand, let alone kiss her. For months he had smiled, charmed, and wooed her, for what? To take her out and spend his money on her for one of her precious smiles. Not even a kiss, although a kiss wouldn't have been nearly enough.

Jesse was so glad he had more irons in the fire than waiting on the Captain's daughter to fall for him so he could have access to Captain Rodriguez's schedule. No need now; his uncle's sources had come through. Uncle Roberto said he would take care of it. Smiling, Jesse thought about how he broke up with the little Ice Princess. It was fun, and he got to mess with her head, gave her something to think about. He recalled how Beauty had gotten up and come looking for him, wanting more of him. He could still feel her soft arms sliding around his neck. Jesse smiled, "Good morning, beautiful. How did you sleep?"

"Sleep was great; waking up was lonely." Jesse's smile turned to a grin; *now, this is a real woman, ready, willing, and able to take care of a man.*

"Well, I think I can help you with the lonely issue," He had pulled her into his arms. The doorbell chimed, causing him to swear under his breath. Then, looking over his shoulder through the sheer covered window, he saw Maria's red Mustang.

"Are you expecting anyone?"

Jesse remembered the little zing he felt when he heard the agitation in her pouty question. A real woman, that's what he wanted, and he was not willing to give up his morning playtime. Jesse decided at that moment to dump Maria. He told Beauty that the little Ice Princess wasn't important, and it felt great to be getting rid of her. He wanted to show her how a real woman treats a man anyway. He walked Beauty closer to the window, gave her a passionate kiss, and then opened the door just enough for Maria to see them. That was sweet! Take that, Ice Princess! Her rosy cheeks showed him that he had hit his mark. The fire he saw in her eyes said it all as she turned without saying a word and walked away. That was a very good day.

≈≈≈

The constant ringing phone pulled Jesse from his deep slumber. His phone would ring, then stop for a brief second, then start again. After the third round, Jesse grabbed the phone, growling, "This had better be important."

"Jesse, we have a situation."

Recognizing his uncle's voice, Jesse set up in bed, wide awake. "Uncle Roberto, what's happened?"

"My contact in the Personnel Department is on administrative leave, pending investigation. She called me this morning; told me she was given an intern on Monday to shadow her for the week. She didn't think anything about it; training interns were a part of her job. Only this intern asked too many questions that most interns shouldn't know. When she got suspicious, she started cleaning up her files, but it was too late. Friday, at the end of the day, she was called in and told she was under investigation for fraud. All of her submissions for promotion are being reviewed. She left the building and went to the airport. So, change of plan, how are you doing with the Captain's daughter?"

"Not good; we broke up."

"Well, you need to fix this; we can't afford to go through anyone else. Go make up with her." Jesse heard the command in his voice.

"She caught me with the Personnel chick."

"Of all the stupid things to do! What were you thinking? Now she can link you to the investigation."

Jesse clenched his jaw, preparing for the tongue lashing to come. At that moment, his phone buzzed, indicating a text from Mrs. Rodriguez. Pausing to read it, he found out that Maria was attacked. Breathing a sigh of relief, he told his uncle that Maria had been attacked over the weekend and, as a result, has lost her short-term memory, that she doesn't remember anything from this past weekend.

"You just got lucky, now go and be everything she needs you to be. We can't move the volume of drugs through that town without having an inside guy."

"Okay, Uncle, but what if she remembers?"

"You need to ask? Kill her." The call ended, allowing Jesse to take a deep breath. He had a bad feeling about this. He didn't like the unknown. This thing with Maria was definitely an unfamiliar place. Jesse knew he would end up killing her; it was just a question of when and how. Maybe he would melt the ice a little before killing her. If she doesn't respond to passion, perhaps she will react to fear. Smiling, he whispered, "Only time will tell, my little Ice Princess."

Chapter Five

Travis Black was bone tired as he walked to his black Suburban truck; who knew there was so much action in a small town? When he accepted the six-month assignment in Resting Place following up on a reliable tip about drugs being trafficked through small off-the-beaten-path towns, he thought it would be pretty easy to spot unusual activity. That was not the case; this town surprised him in more ways than one. The same things motivated the criminals—desires, the lust of the flesh, the lust of the eyes, and the pride of life—so crime happened. The only difference was that the volume was less, but the variety was more than he expected. He and a handful of officers worked to cover all of Resting Place and often helped the smaller towns nearby, like Peace Valley. And then there was the soon to be appointed Chief of Police, Kevin Weston. Travis had never met a humbler man.

During Travis's first week on the job, Kevin invited him to dinner and a basketball game. His brother, Tate, had to work, and he needed a partner to play against his sister, Sidney, and her husband. As it turned out, his brother,

Marcus, and his fiancée joined them as well. After meeting Grams and getting one of the best hugs he'd ever received, he headed out to the backyard court.

Their back yard resembled a picnic area at the park. It was huge, with two picnic tables under a couple of shade trees, a brick grill, and a half-court basketball area.

Stepping on the court, he saw Kevin's sister Sidney cup her hands around her mouth, yelling, "Newbie on the court! Okay, guys, be nice."

Travis had been called many things, but a "newbie" wasn't one, especially in basketball. With his years of college ball and current team ball, he was determined to show what the Newbie could do.

Halfway through the first game, J.P. said, "Hey honey, our Newbie is more skilled than we thought, so scratch that newbie courtesy. Game on!"

The next two games were intense. Sidney and J.P. seem to communicate without words; they just knew where the other was on the court. They appeared to move as one. Travis wondered if he would ever have that kind of relationship. After the second game, they were tied. Kevin walked over to him and said, "Let's switch up, you guard J.P., and I'll take my little sister." Travis smiled when he heard Sidney groan. Kevin and Travis won that game, but the victory was short-lived as Marcus, Sidney's twin brother, and his fiancée took the court.

These two were just as aggressive and in sync as the last. Travis had to tell himself to keep moving; he was so tired that he began missing shots that cost them the game. They all patted him on the back, saying he played a great game. Exhausted, Travis realized that it was a lot of fun playing with these guys. Walking off the backyard court, breathing hard, he said, "You guys are serious about basketball!" They all stopped and looked at him and said, "Yes, we are!" Then they burst out laughing.

Travis looked around and felt it again, home; this felt like home. These guys were really good at basketball, and the women, as beautiful as they were, hustled as hard as the guys. He wondered what it would be like to have a lady like that in his life. Someone with whom he can play ball with, hang out with as well as spoil and love. So far, the women he'd dated were nowhere near that description. If there were only one word to describe the women he'd dated, it was 'more,' always more. Sure, they were beautiful and nice, but as soon as another guy offered them more, they were gone. After a few "Dear John" texts, he pulled back and put dating on the back burner, although his adoptive mother prayed every day for him to find a wife. Feeling his chest tighten with longing at that thought, he pushed the thought away and asked about food, "So what's for dinner?"

≈≈≈

Hearing the station door open, followed by two officers laughing, he pulled his wayward thoughts back to the present. The events of the last few days boggled his mind, a drug lord dead, two officers and a retired officer in custody for attempted murder, and two officers wounded. Shaking his head, he got in his truck and headed to Resting Place Memorial Hospital to check on Kevin, his friend and soon to be his captain.

Chapter Six

Maria sat in the visitor's chair of her hospital room, refusing to lay down any longer. She was frustrated, annoyed, and angry. Why couldn't she remember? She had tried and tried, only gaining a massive headache for her efforts. Her doctor told her that she had psychogenic amnesia, a condition where the brain blocks the memory as a protective measure. The condition was common in trauma cases where the victim had seen or experience extreme trauma. He told her to give it some time, the memories might come back once she returned to her normal routine, but there was a possibility that they may not return.

Maria knew the moment he left that she had work to do. How could she just sit back and give it time? One of her greatest assets was her ability to recall information, to remember details. How could she just give it time? What happened to her? Who beat her like this? How could she not try to remember what happened that day? Had she met Dr. Weston and became friends? *Why would I do that when I'm seeing Jesse?* The more she thought about it, the more her head hurt, and the more exhausted she became. Giving up, for now, she got back in bed. She allowed herself to drift off to sleep, promising that she would work on her memory more after some rest.

≈≈≈

Jesse Mendez stood outside of Maria's hospital room; he was about to deliver the performance of his life. The fact that Maria lost her memory was a lucky break for him. He didn't look forward to wooing the Ice Princess, but he had no choice because of the Personnel issue with Beauty. He had pondered how this situation could work to his advantage for most of the night, and then in the early morning hours, he had a stroke of genius. His uncle Roberto had always told Jesse that there is no great prize without great risk. This project would give him the greatest of prizes.

Jesse smiled as he recalled the day he was summoned to his uncle's office. All the way there, he racked his brain, trying to figure out what he had done to be called in. He had stood in shock as his uncle said, "Nephew, you have served me well all these years. You know I promised your mother that I would take care of you. She would be proud of the man you are today."

His eyes misting a little, Roberto cleared his throat and continued, "You are family, and it's time for you to have something of your own. I am giving you a small project in a small town on the east coast. I'll help you get it set up, and once it produces, you will run it. As you grow, you could own the whole east coast if you handle yourself and your business. Do you want it, son?"

"Yes, Uncle Roberto, I want it." Jesse's smile was huge because, at that moment, his status changed from a nobody to a somebody. That project, better known as "Jesse's Project," was everything to him. Uncle Roberto began showing him the business. In a matter of months, he was revered by some and feared by most. The power was intoxicating and addicting. He loved it—this was the life—and he was not prepared to give it up because of a stuck-up, frigid, self-righteous Ice Princess. Yes, the prize is great. Hence the risk is great. Then it came to him, *what if she thought she was already engaged to me? What would she do? She can't remember. Oh yeah, this could be fun. I just need enough time and opportunity to get our first big delivery, and then we can lay low while we work that through the system.* They needed to get a foot in the door, and the Ice Princess was that door. Jesse allowed himself one more smile before suppressing the joy produced over his plans for Maria. He put on a sympathetic face and walked into the room.

≈≈≈

"Maria, oh baby, I came as soon as I got your Mom's text message." Seeing her bruised face, he worked hard to keep the adoring look while thinking whoever beat her up did a real number on her. She was no beauty now, and maybe never again. Good enough for her. *If things don't go well, this might be your permanent look.* Leaning down, he kissed her right on the lips. He saw her lift her arms in protest before a hand on his shoulder spun him around.

"Get away from her!" Seeing the white coat and name tag, he said, "Oh, Doctor Weston, I'm Jesse Mendez, and I was just greeting my fiancée."

"Wait a minute!" They both spoke at the same time. Maria continued talking while Tate continued staring Jesse down. "What are you talking about, Jesse? We are not engaged."

Tate looked on, wondering if the adoring, concerned looks were fooling Maria. This guy was a piece of work. Deciding his best course of action was to let Maria handle this. She had told

Tate that she had ended the relationship and that she didn't have any feelings for him, but he needed to see if she cared for Jesse. Her initial reaction to him gave Tate hope.

Jesse reached out and took her hand, "Wow, honey; you don't remember? You stopped by last Friday. We hadn't seen each other for a while, so things got kind of serious, and that's when we decided we didn't want to wait to get engaged. Then he reached in his pocket and pulled out a small black box, glad that he stopped at the jewelry store before coming. "I brought this to give to you when you got back in town."

Maria snatched her hands back, folding her arms before replying, "Jesse, this is all too much. I honestly don't remember, so I can't accept your ring. Perhaps in a few days, it will come back to me." Rubbing her temples, she gave a small groan before saying, "Jesse, Dr. Weston, I think I should rest now."

Jesse tried to kiss her forehead, but she moved her head. Tate made an inward sigh; more hope blossomed in his chest. Jesse patted her hand, "I'll see you after my shift tonight."

Maria responded weakly. "Tomorrow is better; all I seem to be able to do is sleep; I think it's the pain medication."

"Okay, see you tomorrow, Princess."

Walking to the parking lot, Jesse applauded his performance; he was in! Even if she didn't believe they were engaged, she wouldn't send him away until she remembered, and by that time, his little empire will have already been established.

Chapter Seven

Tate hesitated before leaving; he wanted to make sure Mendez left. He didn't like that guy. He was lying to her face. He knew they were not engaged. Why would he lie about it? Why is he still trying to be with her when he wanted to get rid of her last Friday? Making a mental note to talk with Kevin, Ben, or Trace to check this guy out. He turned his attention back to Maria. "Ms. Rodriguez, I'm sorry I interrupted…"

Before Tate could finish, Maria said, "No, you're not."

He allowed himself a small grin; he loved her direct, upfront approach to everything. At first, it had caught him off guard, but once they started talking, he found that he liked her frankness; he didn't have to worry about guessing what she was thinking. This woman had no problems telling you.

"You didn't look comfortable with his greeting; I just wanted to make sure you were safe."

Maria looked at him through lowered lashes, "Thank you."

Tate couldn't stop himself from saying. "I guess I should congratulate you on your engagement." Tate wasn't smiling.

Tate saw the fire ignite in her eyes before she said, "Dr. Weston, I may have lost some of my memory, but I haven't lost my mind! I do remember talking with my parents and deciding that I was going to end our relationship. So, the way I see it, at worst, we are still dating, and at best, at least for me, we are no longer dating. Regardless, we are definitely not engaged."

Tate couldn't contain the smile that came across his face. "If you don't mind, I want my brother to check Mendez out. Lying about your relationship with him is a concern, a red flag that's worth looking into."

"Please do. I would feel better about it. I will also ask my father to check on him. He's one of our newer police officers, less than a year."

Noticing her eyes heavy with sleep, Tate walked over and leaned over her and said, "Look, Maria, I know this is a lot for you; don't try to force the memories. They will come in time."

She spoke so softly he knew she was already slipping into sleep. Leaning closer, he heard her say, "What if they don't come back?"

"Then, we'll make new memories, Maria." Brushing her hair off her face, he prayed for her and left her room. He pulled out his phone, made two calls, one to Ben Rayns and another to Tony Rodriguez.

≈≈≈

After visiting Maria, Tate wanted to talk with Kevin but wasn't sure if the time was right, Kevin was home recuperating. His shoulder was fine, and with time and rest, he would make a full recovery and be back at work, training for his new position as the Chief of Resting Place Police Department.

Tate had tried not to talk about Maria, but Kevin knew something was going on with him. They were very close friends as well as brothers. Over the years, Tate had seen many different sides of his brother, even the parental side, when he was out of line and needed a firm hand. Earlier that evening, Tate had seen that parental side as he tried to get away with an excuse that he needed to stop by the hospital and check on a patient.

Kevin had asked, "Which patient Tate? I know Maria is scheduled for discharge in the next couple of days, so who else are you checking on after visiting hours?"

Tate felt like a kid caught in a lie, and then he had seen the concern in his brother's eyes and a slight smile lifting the corner of his lip. "She'll be discharged tomorrow, and okay, something happened between Maria and me at Safe Haven. We discovered that we liked each other, really liked each other, and had plans to see each other after the assignment, but now she doesn't remember anything from that weekend."

"Wow, Tate, I know this must be hard for you. How are you seeing her now if she doesn't remember you?"

"It's weird because she doesn't remember, but then she will do something that she did with me, then get frustrated because she doesn't remember. I want to tell her about it, but I know I need to be patient and with Jesse Mendez claiming to be engaged to her." Tate realized too late that he had said more than he wanted.

"Who is Jesse Mendez?"

"Maria's ex-boyfriend, the problem is, she broke up with him over the weekend..."

"And doesn't remember." Kevin had finished the thought. "I get it, so now Mendez is trying to get back with her?"

"Something like that, but even without her memory, she's not buying the engagement story."

Kevin started to say something but stopped and looked at Tate. Then a big grin covered his face, "You're in love. Wow, little brother, I knew it would happen one day. God is so funny! Indeed, He has a sense of humor. The guy who has had a padlock on his heart with a do not disturb sign on the lock has fallen in love in one day! I can't wait the tell J.P. and Marcus about this!"

"Come on, Kevin…"

"No can do, little brother. You ribbed me and teased me mercilessly over Lilly. It's my turn, and I intend to enjoy every moment of this. So, get ready. We have a game night next week. I won't be able to play, but I wouldn't miss that night for the world." Then he patted Tate on the shoulder with his good arm and said, "Tate, all joking aside, I am happy for you, and I can't wait to meet Maria. God didn't give you this incredible love for no reason. He's got a plan. Trust Him. He will guide you and Maria through this. Oh, and in the meantime, I will check out this Mendez guy. It's just a feeling, but something doesn't seem right with what you have shared. It won't hurt to check him out."

"Thanks, Kevin, rest that shoulder. I'll be back a little later."

Chapter Eight

With only a few minutes before he was needed in the ER, Tate stood looking down at Maria's sleeping form. The fading bruises on her face still caused the guilt to twist in his gut. He couldn't protect her. Never in his life had he felt so helpless. *And now she doesn't even remember me. Father, what now? How do we get back to where we were? Will she ever remember me? Father, what now? Will she care about me again? I don't want to walk away from her.*

Gently taking her right hand, he prayed quietly. "Father, in the name of Jesus. I lift Maria up to you today. I pray for healing in her body. Heal her completely spirit, soul, emotions, and body. Father protect her with your angels, and Holy Spirit bring back to her remembrance what she can't remember. I declare the enemy will not steal these memories from her in Jesus' name. Oh, and Father, remind Maria that you are in control and that she can trust You with this process."

≈≈≈

Maria let out a breath and opened her eyes after Dr. Weston left her hospital room. Playing possum as a kid with her three brothers had helped her on a few cases when the stillness was the only defense she had. Today it took everything in her to remain still as Dr. Weston prayed over her. He asked God if she would remember him. Who was this guy? He talked with God as if he knew her and knew her well, and cared for her. *God, who is he to me? What happened last Friday? And why do I feel sparks whenever he touches me? Why do I feel safe with him?*

Maria moved from the bed to the chair next to it, picked up her journal, and began writing down everything she could remember. One hour later, she had a massive headache and a huge smile. She remembered something! She remembered the drive to Jesse's house and her determination to end their relationship. Maria was so excited that she could remember something that she grabbed her phone and sent a quick text to her mom and dad. A couple of minutes later, her phone rang her father's face on the screen. Her dad started talking, "Praise God! Honey, that's great news!" Her mom chimed in, "Oh, Maria! This is wonderful news, baby! Thank you, Jesus! Thank you, God!"

Maria's dad shifted into police mode, asking what she remembered, jotting down what she said, reminding her that it's okay, and calm down when he heard in her voice that she was straining to remember more. Maria also told him of Jesse's visit and this supposed engagement. They were as shocked as she had been when she heard it. Tony looked at his wife and asked, "You said Dr. Weston was in the room? What were his thoughts?" Maria thought about the incident and said, "He looked shocked because he yanked Jesse off of me. Jessie was trying to kiss me. I know we had not progressed to that point. So, I was glad Dr. Weston was here. Thank God. I wondered if he knew Jesse. He seems like he did, but my head was pounding by then, and I wanted Jesse gone. Dr. Weston said he was going to talk with his brother about checking Jesse out, so he might give you a call as well."

Tony Rodriguez smiled and said he would look for Dr. Weston's call. Hearing how drained Maria had become, her dad led them into prayer, thanking God for this great blessing and asking for her complete healing. "Get some rest, baby girl; we'll see you in the morning."

Maria's mom added, "We love you, sweet girl." Feeling exhausted but happy, Maria got in the bed and drifted off to sleep.

≈≈≈

Tate stood outside Maria's hospital room. Her discharge was scheduled for the next day, and he still hadn't asked if he could visit her at home while she recovered. He was nervous, really nervous, like heart-pounding, sweaty palms nervous. She always addressed him as Dr. Weston. He would catch her staring at him, obviously frustrated that she didn't remember him, and even more frustrated because she didn't understand her reactions to him.

Hearing harsh voices in her room, Tate pushed the door open to find Maria and Jesse in a standoff. He immediately moved between them and noticed a red handprint on Jesse's face. Before he could say anything, Jesse's phone ranged. He looked at it and then back at Maria and said, "We'll finish this later."

Maria snapped back, "It's already finished. Don't come near me again, Officer Mendez." Maria stared him out the door.

As soon as the door closed, she grabbed Tate, pulled him close, and started telling him what happened. Her actions instantly took him back to Safe Haven, where they shared their secrets. He was momentarily overwhelmed, being close to her again until he focused on what she was saying about Jesse trying to kiss her and not accepting her "no." Tate pulled her closer and said, "That will never happen again!" His anger was so intense he could barely speak.

Then Maria pulled away from him, surprise on her face, saying more to herself, "What am I doing?" Taking a few steps away from him, she looked in his eyes, then rubbed her temples as if in pain.

Feeling helpless, Tate said, "Can I get you something for pain?"

"No, but you can tell me, Dr. Weston, who are you to me?"

Tate hesitated, though her memory was coming back slowly, her doctor had cautioned him not to press her with too much information. He did say that he could answer questions if she asked, but seeing her in pain, he knew now wasn't the time to talk about what they had shared. "We were or are friends."

"Is that all we are, Dr. Weston? Tate?"

She said his name; it was the first time she said it, and it was almost his undoing. He wanted to tell her about their incredible time together. But he would not push. *God give me the patience to wait until she is truly ready to hear or until she remembers.*

"Maria now is not a good time to continue this discussion. You're in pain and need to get some rest. I'll stop by and visit you in a few days if that's okay?"

"Okay, I'll get some rest, but until you answer my question, there is no need for you to visit me." Then, lifting her cute chin in defiance, she got in his face and asked again, "Is that all we are, friends?"

Chapter Nine

Tate stared into her honey-brown eyes, accented with fire, and lost the battle. Reaching for her, he closed the last few inches that separated them and kissed her. When his lips touched hers, an explosion of joy and light and colors erupted inside of him. He didn't want to scare her and tried to pull back, but she pulled him closer and kissed him more deeply. It took every ounce of willpower he possessed to end that kiss. Pulling away from her, he whispered in her ear, "No, Maria, we are more than friends. I will give you a call later." Then turned and walked out of the room.

Maria stood in the middle of the floor, tingling; every part of her was affected by that kiss. She'd never experienced anything like that; in fact, up until that moment, she didn't even like kissing. That's how she knew she hadn't kissed Jesse and would not allow him to touch her again. As she touched her lips, she realized her headache was gone.

≈≈≈

Tate stood outside of Chief Rodriguez's office, frustrated every time he thought about Jesse trying to force Maria; his anger spiked anew. It had taken him a walk outside to clear his head after kissing Maria; his heart was beating out of his chest as hope grew within him. She might not remember him, but what they had shared, the connection was still present. When he could think about something other than Maria, his thoughts went to Jesse. The idea of him trying to hurt Maria caused him to feel emotions that he only experienced in the form of nightmares. He knew that the rage he felt when Jesse walked in and kissed Maria after she'd awaken was a problem, so he had talked with both Uncle Ben and Chief Rodriguez about Jesse; they both were checking him out. He also felt better after talking with Kevin, but now, just thinking about Jesse near Maria put him in a whole other head space.

Chief Rodriguez had talked with Jesse and asked that he give Maria some time to recover. That request fell on deaf ears, and that bothered Tate too. Everything about Jesse Mendez bothered Tate. He'd seen the look in Jesse's eyes. He would have hurt Maria and enjoyed doing it. She would have fought him, but in her weakened state, she was at a disadvantage. Tate had almost gone after him, but the Holy Spirit led him to her dad. Knocking on the door, he entered the room.

Tony Rodriguez looked up from a folder on his desk, seeing the stormy look on Tate's face, asked, "What's wrong?"

"Mendez, he tried to kiss Maria when she told him no, he tried to force his way."

Tony listened. Every word Tate spoke enraged him more. When he questioned Tate, his voice was quiet, dangerously quiet, "Did he hurt her? Is my daughter okay?"

Tate was quick to add, "She is okay, mad as fire. I walked in before Jesse could do anything." Before he could respond, another knock sounded on his door. At his call to come in, Ben Rayns and Officer Travis Black walked in.

≈≈≈

Jesse sat in his living room, rubbing his cheek; it still stung, that little vixen. If that goodie-two-shoes doctor hadn't interrupted them, she would have paid for that slap. Then the call from his uncle made him forget about his face.

Their shipment was coming into town at the end of the week, Friday. His time had run out; he had no idea what the Captain's schedule would be and no way of finding out. *Think Jesse. Think, there has got to be another way. What can I do? How can I control this situation?*

He got up, pacing around the room, pondering what to do. Then a wide grin spread across his face. *I know exactly where all the policemen in Peace Valley will be that night. They will be looking for the captain's daughter, and before they find her, the little Ice Princess will have a meltdown.*

Smirking, he picked up his phone and called his uncle. A half-hour later, their plan was in place. Jesse hung up with his uncle and called a couple of his men to grab Maria and hide her away somewhere until he could get to her. He gave them Maria's address.

His last call was to his contact for the delivery. The warehouse was ready. Everything was in place. His uncle was happy with the plan, and Jesse was looking forward to the end of the week! He was excited. By this time next week, he would own this town.

Chapter Ten

Officer Travis Black walked into Mason's Diner; since they would close soon, he would get takeout and maybe catch a game on TV. He was surprised when a tall, beautiful, curvaceous African American woman approached him and said, "Hey babe, you're early tonight. Come on back while I get my purse." Looking into his eyes, she mouthed the word *help*.

That was all that Travis needed to see. Moving close, sliding his arm around her waist, he leaned in and whispered in her ear. "Who are we talking about?" She giggled and stood on tiptoes with her hands on his shoulders.

"The two in the booth to the far right. Take a look, then follow me in the back." He looked around and saw the men grinning at him; one even lifted his mug of beer in salute.

Travis took in as many details as he could without staring for identification, then said, "Come on, darling, let's get that purse."

Once they entered the back of the restaurant, Susie let out a breath and told him what she'd heard while sitting a few booths away working on the payroll. "The taller one said that they have a new assignment. We need to snatch some lady cop and hold her until the Boss can get to her, then we can load the cargo, collect our pay, and we're out of here. The other guy asked why snatch the girl? He said she is the distraction, and he wants to have some fun with her."

Travis knew who and what they were talking about. He pulled out his phone and called Captain Smith, who got Ben Rayns on the line. Susie moved to her desk and began packing up to leave. Travis could see she was nervous and perceived concern in her eyes. Hanging up, he moved over to her and said, "You know, when I walked in and got that very warm reception, I thought my winning smile had worked its magic on you." Then he winked to let her know he was kidding. Her blush was unexpected and appealing. He cleared his throat and continued, "We need to make them believe that we are so into each other that they don't get suspicious. Are you up for that?"

Hearing her quiet consent, he said, "By the way, my name is Travis Black. You may have seen me; I come here mostly on my days off, usually for dinner."

Susie smiled, held out her hand, and said, "Hi Travis. I am glad to meet you, I'm sorry for approaching you like we have something between us, but I didn't know how else to get close enough to you to tell you what was happening."

Taking a breath to stop herself from rambling, she continued, "I'm Susan Mason. Everyone calls me Susie. This is my family's restaurant. I handle the accounting and help out when needed."

Travis held her hand while she talked, noticing tiny tingles moving up his arm. Then he said, "It's nice to meet you, Susan." Smiling at her, he cleared his throat. "I am going to walk you to your car, kiss you, then follow you home, and make sure you get inside safely." Seeing that blush again, he asked, "Is that okay?" She nodded her agreement; then they left the room arm in arm.

Susie Mason walked beside Travis Black wondering if she had done the right thing approaching him like that. She already had a bad reputation; grabbing a stranger, kissing in the parking lot wasn't going to make things any better. Try as she might, she couldn't live down the fact that she dated T.J. Muller. She hadn't known all the lies he had spread around town about her. By the time she found out just how bad the picture he had painted of her, it was too late. The damage was done.

If the truth were told, she had gone out with T.J. twice, and nothing, not even a kiss on the cheek, happened. No one would believe her; she had no choice but to live it down. Hard to do after today, but again she had no choice. That lady, whoever she was, might be in serious danger. If this helped her, Susie's reputation would be okay.

She glanced over and up to see Travis Black watching her. He was one of the good guys like Kevin, but unlike Kevin, Travis' smile stole her breath and his touch evoked tingles. She liked Kevin, but she didn't love him. She wanted real love, heart-stopping, breathtaking, toe-curling love, and as much as she liked Kevin, she knew that she didn't love him. Their breakup resulted from Kevin seeing her with T.J. –strike one; the rumors T.J. spread –strike two; then T.J. shooting Kevin and being arrested –strike three. Susie could feel tears near the surface, so she dropped her head, took a breath, and kept walking, telling herself it would be over soon, and she can go home and have a good cry.

When they reached the car, Travis turned her to face him. He looked into her eyes then lowered his head. He intended to give her a gentle kiss, hug her, and tuck her into her car. That did not happen; once his lips touched hers, the sensation was so intense that he couldn't pull away. Then she gave him a soft sigh and kissed him back. Never had Travis experienced what he was feeling. Pulling back, he whispered, "Susan, I'm not sure what just happened, but I would really like to talk about it later. Is that okay?" He felt her nod her head in agreement. "Good. He helped her into her car, leaned in, kissed her cheek, closed the door, and ran to his truck.

Susie drove home checking her rearview mirror every few minutes. That kiss was certainly heart-stopping, mindblowing, and a few other words she couldn't think of right now. What did he mean? He would like to talk about what happened. Wasn't that a part of his job? Wasn't he acting? If he was going to tell her he was just doing his job, she didn't want to hear it. Well, she wasn't acting, and in a matter of minutes, she had experienced what she had been waiting her whole life to feel. Wow, and it was with someone who was acting, just doing his job. God, help me! She arrived home, ran into the house, and wave at Travis Black as he drove away.

Chapter Eleven

Travis walked beside Ben Rayns entering Peace Valley's Police precinct, his thoughts back in the parking lot of Mason's Diner. *Lord, what just happened? I know Susan approached me the way that she did to gain my help. I get that, but when we touched and when we kissed, it felt like more; it felt like we connected. Lord, You know what I long for in a relationship, in a marriage, and I've asked you to choose for me. Could Susan be Your choice? Father, if she is the one for me, give me a sign.*

Thinking about the time he spent playing basketball with Kevin's family, how their wives played with them, Travis wanted that; he wanted a wife to share the things that he loved and the things she loved. *Father, if she loves You and can play basketball with me, I'll know.*

Travis remembered how elegant, how beautiful Susan looked at the restaurant. She wore black straight-leg jeans that dipped down into black leather ankle boots and a soft lace pink top. She was classy, and he had liked the way she walked up to him and claimed him with a single word, *babe.* Shaking his head to clear that picture, he scolded himself. No way she would play basketball with him or go out with him. Better to start getting her out of his system because that classy beauty had, without any effort, already gotten too close to his battered heart.

"Travis, I understand you have some information about a large supply of drugs coming into town."

Travis responded to Chief Rodriguez's question, "Our sources informed us that the drugs are due in later this week, but I found out tonight how they plan to move them in. Susan Mason overheard a couple of guys talking about snatching a lady cop and holding till their boss can get to her."

Both chief and Dr. Weston sprang to their feet, talking at the same time. "I'm going over there right now."

Pulling out his phone, Tate called one of his colleagues to cover him in the ER for the rest of the week. No way will he let anything happen to Maria. Through his racing thoughts, he heard Uncle Ben, "Tate, there's more. Calm down and listen, son."

Tate took a couple of deep breaths to calm himself, nodding at Uncle Ben to continue. "Kevin called me right before Travis did and informed me that he checked on Mendez after talking with you. He found out that this Mendez guy doesn't exist. He showed up in Peace Valley about eight months ago. He had his file pulled, did more digging, and found out that he is the nephew of Hector and Roberto Ramos."

Travis spoke quietly following Marshall Rayns' lead, watching Chief Tony Rodriguez and Dr. Weston's murderous looks. "Jesse Ramos was sent to establish a distribution base in Peace Valley. His job on the police force provides him with the perfect cover when moving drugs. This guy has been under the radar for some time; we had no clue who was the point man until Ben was asked to check out Jesse Mendez."

Ben picked up where Travis left off, "If we handle this right, we can cut the head off this snake."

Tony Rodriguez spoke up, "What are you talking about, Ben?"

"Tony, I know you would rather go after these guys right now, but if we show our hand, they may pick up on it and bolt. If we let it play out, then we could round up everybody involved with the drugs. That will bring enough heat and attention to Peace Valley to keep anyone from setting up shop here again."

Tony considered what Ben proposed, then asked, "What about Maria? I don't want her in any danger."

Ben smiled and said, "I bet you wouldn't say that to her face."

Tony laughed out loud, "No, I wouldn't, she'd take my head off! But I want her safe." Looking at Tate.

Tate responded, "I will keep her safe, Tony." They stared at each other until Tony said, "Okay, what's the plan?"

Ben said, "First we pray, then we plan. Tony, why don't you check on your family? Let them know you will have some company for the next few days." Tony was dialing the number before Ben finished talking.

Chapter Twelve

Maria openly stared at Tate and her dad talking, wondering what was going on. Even her mother seems to have fallen under Dr. Weston's spell, laughing at his jokes, blushing at his compliments. They like him; dad liked him. She liked him too. Okay, she more than liked him and blushed every time she thought about the kiss they shared. Closing her eyes, she silently prayed, *Father, something good happened between us. I feel like I know him, I respond to him, and he acts like he really cares for me. Father, please help me remember what happened between us. In Jesus Name. Amen.*

"Hey, are you okay?"

Maria knew his voice, "Hey Tate. So, dad said, you are spending a few days with us. Why?"

Tate meant to evade her question, but looking into her honey-brown eyes, he felt a boldness to tell her how he felt.

"Because I miss you. Because I have spent every day with you since the day we met. Because I love to hear you laugh, and seeing your smile makes me happy. Because the day we spent together was the best day of my entire life. Because what we shared changed me. It made me dream. Maria, I know you don't remember, but I do, and I can't walk away from you. I care too much. Because that look you are giving me right now lets me know that what we have is real...." Stepping closer, Tate held her face in his hands and whispered, "You are the most beautiful woman I have ever seen." Then he kissed her.

Maria listened to everything Tate said, each word softening her heart. She had googled him and found out a lot of information about him and his accomplishments. She had a lot of data on Dr. Tate Weston, but she knew instinctively that he was sharing with her a side of himself that no one else was privy. Yet, he shared that part of himself with her. That made her feel special, precious, treasured... loved. *He loves me! He loves me! And I love him. I don't remember, but I know that I loved him because I am falling in love with him all over again. When he touched my face and told me that I was the most beautiful woman he had ever seen, he wasn't looking at the bruises; he was looking at me! He sees me! And he loves me! Oh God, what a wonderful gift this man is.*

In that split-second, Maria knew that she wanted Tate Weston in her life even if she didn't remember. She wanted to spend her life with this man. She would not even try to remember what they had; she would focus on what they could have. Her mother was right; love will make you willing to make adjustments. She was more than willing and happy to do it. She knew that from this moment on, her life would never be the same. When he kissed her, and she released her heart to Tate Weston.

Pulling away, breathless, they both said, "Wow." Then Tate looked into her eyes and asked, "Maria, what just happened? Something changed. I felt it."

Maria, feeling so much and afraid that she read him wrong, dropped her head, blushing profusely. "Nothing, it's nothing."

Sensing her fear, Tate lifted her chin and said, "Come here." He pulled her close, not saying anything, just holding her until she settled down and peace seeped into her. Then he said, "Tell me."

After a long pause, she sighed and said, "I don't remember anything else, but I know I loved you before because I love… realizing what she was saying, she stopped and started pulling away.

Tate tightened his hold just enough to cause her to look at him. "Maria, I love you. He kissed her lightly on the lips, then her nose, then her eyes.

Between kisses, she whispered, "I love you too, Tate."

≈≈≈

Tony Rodriguez cleared his throat as he walked into the room, "Maria, your mother needs your help preparing Dr. Weston's room for the night."

"Yes, Daddy." Before leaving the room, she turned to Tate with a heart-stopping smile, then rushed out of the room. Tate felt the immediate shift in the room, going from warm and cozy to tense.

Tony spoke quietly, "Does she remember?"

Tate shook his head before saying, "No, sir, she doesn't remember."

"Then, Dr. Weston, I believe you have captured my daughter's heart again. What are your intentions?"

"Sir, we haven't known each other for very long, but I love Maria, and with your permission, I would like to court her and, in the near future, ask her to marry me." Tate had no idea where all this boldness was coming from, but there it was. All his cards were on the table, and he was going to stand his ground.

Tony took so long to respond that Tate thought he was going to ignore him. His palms were sweating, and he was trying to remember if he had said anything to offend her father.

"Tate, I see the way my daughter lights up when you come into the room; she reminds me of her mother when we first met. My wife and I give you our blessings to court our daughter and get to know our family. We are very close, and I would rather gain a son than lose a daughter. I believe you love her, and I believe she cares deeply for you. Rosa and I will be praying for you both.

Chapter Thirteen

Travis scanned Mason's restaurant from his corner booth. He had seen the two men when he walked in and sent a text to Ben once he was seated.

He asked the waitress who approached him with the name Julie on her badge if Susan was in today. Julie smiled and informed him that Susie was in the office, and she would let her know that he wanted to see her.

Travis knew from the smiles and knowing looks that word had gotten around that Susan might have a boyfriend. He smiled at the thought of Susan Mason being his girlfriend. That triggered thoughts of their kiss in the parking lot, and his smile grew bigger.

The buzzing from Travis' phone stopped his daydreaming. While reading the text from Ben, Susan walked over to his table. Travis pocketed his phone, stood up, giving her a lingering hug. He whispered in her ear, "I need to get some pictures of the booth. Are you up for some selfies?"

She giggled, and Travis couldn't help, nuzzling her neck and breathing in the coconut scent he now associated with Susan. Hearing her sigh only encouraged him. Pulling back, grinning, he said, "Ms. Mason, we can't keep meeting this way!" Then he winked at her.

She giggled again and said, "Why Mr. Black, you need to tone down that winning smile, or you might just turn a girl's head." She was flirting! What was she thinking? She was flirting with Travis Black!

Then his smile kicked up in full force. Warning bells went off in Susan's head, letting her know that this man is dangerous to her heart.

Travis had an odd mix of curly raven black hair and sky-blue eyes, tall and lean. He was a Native American, standing six-foot, three inches tall, and all muscle. He made her feel feminine even though she was five feet, seven inches, and more curvaceous than most women. She felt safe around him; she also realized she was still in his arms, and it felt really good, too good.

Cheeks heated, she cleared her throat and stepped back. "Yes, selfies, let's do that!"

For the next 10 minutes, they took selfies and pictures of the men in the booth to send Ben Rayns. Halfway through their selfies, Susie questioned her sanity as she smiled, hugged, kissed, and made funny faces with Travis Black.

He asked Susan for her cell number, sent her the selfies, and sent some pictures to Ben Rayns.

When she stood to return to her office, Travis asked in a quiet, almost shy voice, "Have dinner with me tonight?"

Their eyes met, and she saw it, with uncertainty and hope Travis was asking her out. She shouldn't; she knew a relationship with him would end the moment the rumors started. Her reputation would destroy any possibilities of a relationship with him, but that look in his eyes called to a deep place inside of her, and she couldn't deny the call. She responded, leaning forward in a low voice, "For real?"

Travis smiled, "Yes, for real, I have a feeling work is going to get very busy in the next few days. I'm off tonight, and I would like to take you out." Travis stopped talking; he was rambling.

"Yes, what time should I be ready?"

Letting out a breath and smiling, he said, "I can pick you up after work. What time do you get off?"

"Actually, I'm only working till noon today."

Looking at his watch, noticing that it was currently 11:30 a.m., he asked, "Are you done? Did I interrupt something you need to finish?"

"No, I just need to clean up my desk."

"Great! I'll finish my coffee while you do that, and then we can leave."

Travis watched her walk back to her office, thanking God for the chance to spend more time with the very beautiful Susan Mason.

≈≈≈

Travis was in trouble; this woman was perfect! They had spent almost all day together, and he was trying to come up with something to give him more time with her.

They had talked a lot, and he found that he liked talking with Susan. He usually listened more than talk, but Susan didn't have any problem asking him about himself, family, and friends. She didn't mind waiting for an answer while he pondered what to say. Travis liked that, and he liked her a lot. He could envision a life with Susan; he was falling and falling fast.

"Why do you call me Susan?"

Susan's question pulled him from his thoughts. Surprised she'd asked, he stalled, "Why do I call you Susan? That's your name, right?"

Giving him a playful look that didn't completely cover her disappointment, she responded, "When we met, I told you my name was Susan, but my friends call me Susie. You still call me Susan. Why?"

Travis considered her words and the look she gave him before responding, "To me, Susan suits you. Whenever I think about you, your name Susan comes to mind. If you prefer, I can call you Susie, but Susan suits you from everything I have learned about you so far. And I like the name." He smiled and asked, "Can I call you Susan?"

Susan smiled back at him, wondering if he knew how his words had affected her. Not just his words but the way he looked into her eyes as if she was the only woman in the room. No one had ever looked at her that way. And when he said her name, it felt special. Her toes were curling, and the man hadn't even touched her. Taking a deep breath, she answered, "Sure, Susan is okay."

Travis smiled and said, "Thanks," as the waitress approached with dessert menus.

After dessert, Travis stood. Taking Susan's hand, he asked her if she would like to take a walk to a nearby park.

"Do you think I need the exercise, Officer Black?"

Travis could tell he had offended Susan. He allowed his eyes to travel from her almond-shaped brown eyes to her pink sparkly sneakers with an appreciation of what he saw before responding, "No, ma'am, you do not need to exercise."

Susan's blush let him know that he got his message across. "Come on. I want to play some basketball with you."

"Wait a minute; you're asking me to play basketball with you on our first date?"

Travis' stomach dropped; *okay, here it comes.* "Can you play?"

Susan burst out laughing, "Can I play? I got my MBA on a basketball scholarship and coached a girls' basketball team at Peace Valley Community Church. Can I Play?"

Her indignant snort caused him to laugh out loud.

"Okay, let's play, and the loser takes the winner out for a steak dinner and dessert."

Travis was done, totally captivated! Win, lose, or draw; he knew he would never be the same. He drove back to Mason's Diner, where Susan parked her car and retrieved a pink gym bag and a basketball.

Travis couldn't stop grinning while playing ball with Susan until they were tied one game each, and she was two points ahead of him. The girl could play some basketball.

Truth be told, he was too busy watching how she handle the ball, the way she got in his face trying to take his ball. She played just as hard as those Weston women. She was terrific, and he decided playing basketball with Susan was at the top of the list of his favorite things to do.

Getting his head into the game, Travis won the game by two hard-won points. "Wow! Where did you learn to play ball?" He asked.

"I have three brothers; I was the only girl. I had to be good, so they would let me play." Beaming, she said, "Okay, when and where. I owe you a steak!"

Travis' heart was beating out of his chest. "Tomorrow night. I get off at 6:00 p.m. I'll pick you up at 7:30 p.m."

Susan frowned as she said, "No way, my treat, I'll pick you up at 7:30."

Travis started to object, but she stopped him with a no-nonsense look that he knew she used with the girls she coached.

"Look, Travis, if you ever want to play ball with me again, we'll have to honor the rules of the game."

Seeing how serious she was, he conceded. "Okay, 7:30 p.m."

Travis followed her home after their game, wishing he had thought to suggest that they drop off her car before going to the park. After spending most of the day with Susan, he found that he didn't want their time together to end. Walking her to her door, he pulled her into his arms and kissed her until they were breathless before walking away, "Goodnight, Susan, see you tomorrow."

Susie walked into the house in a daze; as she headed to her bedroom, her phone buzzed, indicating a text. "Susan, thank you for spending the day with me. I had an amazing time and am looking forward to having dinner with you tomorrow."

Grinning, Susie texted, "I had an amazing time too, thank you. Looking forward to dinner too!" Her smile grew as she added a smiley face to her text. Plopping down on her bed, she couldn't stop smiling. Thinking over the events of the day with Travis, she decided that this was the best day of her entire life. When thoughts about the rumors drifted in, she pushed them back, holding on to the dream of Travis for a little longer.

Chapter Fourteen

Jesse was happier than he ever remembered being. Everything was in place. The shipment was on track due to arrive tomorrow around midnight--check! The Ice Princess, on track, his boys had located the house and verified she was there—check! Customers had already placed their orders—check! Uncle Roberto is happy with the plan—check!

As Jesse checked off his mental list, his grin grew bigger. By next week, he will be well established in this quaint little town, and business will be thriving!

Pulling out his phone, he called his contact to confirm the package delivery time. "Hunter. Hey man, are we good to go?"

A very cultured baritone voice came over the phone. "Yes, everything is in place. The warehouse has been prepared. You can use it for 30 days; then, I'll relocate the merchandise to another location in another small town. Remember, we will not disclose the location until the day of the transfer."

"I got it." Jesse didn't like this guy. Hunter always talked down to him, acting like he was so much better than him, always pointing out faults, saying the devil is in the details. The previous month when they had met with Uncle Roberto, the jerk tried to show him up. That was a fatal mistake, and once this job was finished, Mr. high-class Hunter Stevenson would have an unfortunate fatal accident. Smiling at the thought, Jesse softened his tone and said, "Yeah, I got it. Thanks for the reminder."

Hunter Stevenson hung up the phone, smirking. Jesse was such an easy target; goading him and insulting him was fun, and Jesse was playing right into his hands.

Jesse's uncle had ruled his people with fear, and Jesse had learned this technique well, but to rule this new empire required brains, something Jesse was in short supply. *So the bait is laid, the trap is set; now, all we need is the mouse.*

Hunter smiled as he remembered his dad telling him to stay on the football team because he wasn't smart enough to go to college any other way. Although Hunter was big, he was very smart but too afraid to tell his dad that he was more than a dumb jock. Nowadays, he was worth millions and soon to be worth billions, and he had earned it all with his brain, not his brawn. Hunter's smile grew at the thought of taking over Jesse's project. It was the sweetest kind of victory when he gains wealth off of someone else stupidity!

Hunter's ringing phone drew his attention. Seeing his dad's picture on the screen, he shook his head before answering. "Hey, Dad. I thought I asked you to text instead of calling." He put a little frost in his voice.

"I know, son. You did, but I haven't figured out how to use the texting thing yet."

"Okay, Dad, I'll show you again when I come for a visit next week."

"Thanks, son. Mom wanted me to call to see if you had sent the check. She wants to do some shopping."

"Tell Mom the money should be in the account tomorrow. Okay, Dad, I got to go." Hunter hung up before his dad could ask for anything else. He remembered fearing his father as a young boy and even as a teenager, but after he moved away to attend college, he began to see that he wasn't the stupid one. His dad was the big dumb jock, and having to teach him how to text for the third time only proved his point. Hunter despised his father. That was why he always delayed putting money into their bank account; he wanted his dad to ask for it. Dad asking him for money made him feel powerful and in control, two things he'd never experienced as a boy with his Dad. The $300.00 he gave them each month was a small price to hear his Dad almost beg for it. Once this deal worked out for him, he might consider increasing their funds to $350.00. Snickering at the thought of how little he gave them, he put his phone away.

Chapter Fifteen

Tate marveled at the peace he felt working on Maria's 1965 fire engine red Mustang. The car was in excellent condition, and the few imperfections he noticed the day they met were fixed, bringing her car to mint condition. He smiled as he looked over to his restored Oldsmobile 442.

Maria loved Tate's car and wanted to drive it! He never let anyone operate his cars; most of his friends and family didn't even ask. Yet, when Maria asked, he could envision her in the driver's seat and wanted to create that memory with her. Putting her off, he said they could take a ride together over the weekend, and maybe she could drive. The squeal she gave was one of pure joy! Tate knew by the intense satisfaction he felt by making her happy that he would do anything in his power to make that happen.

Tate was grinning like a fool, but he couldn't help it. Maria agreed to courtship, and after they catch Mendez, they would have their first date. Bowing his head, he prayed. *Father, I am so very grateful to you! Thank you for Maria agreeing to see me, and she doesn't remember but still cares for me! God, Thank you! Help me keep her safe this weekend.*

Give all of us wisdom during this time. Show us the plans of the enemy. Please keep the Rodriguez family safe and Lord, give Maria wisdom as well. I know she is trained to take care of herself. If it comes to that, God give her wisdom. Feeling God's peace, Tate returned to the Mustang, rushing to finish up before Maria came looking for him and ruin his surprise.

≈≈≈

"Are your eyes closed?" Tate teased as he guided her out to the garage with his hands over her eyes. Maria, more than bothered by his nearness, resisted the urge to call him Dr. Weston. Since their last conversation, he told her how much it bothered him when she called him Dr. Weston as if there were nothing between them. She understood, but the urge was growing. She hated surprises.

"Dude! How am I supposed to see with your big hands over my eyes?" Then an idea came to her, oh yeah, two could play this game. Softening her voice, she said, "Nice, capable hands....." Hearing Tate take a quick intake of breath, she continued, "And very strong arms...."

Tate's voice was hoarse when he spoke, "Maria, unless you plan to marry me today, you need to stop playing with me." Amazed at the effect she had on him, she giggled and leaned back against his chest. "Maria, you really need to stop…." Leaning in, he nuzzled her neck, breathing in her scent.

Quickly leaning forward, Maria said, "Tate. Tate. Tate!" Pushing him away, she said, "Tate, I'm sorry, I shouldn't have done that. I've never acted like that before, and I know and share your commitment to purity. Please forgive me?"

Tate immediately released Maria, realizing how consumed he was this close to her. He took several deep breaths to clear his head enough to apologize for his behavior and to assure her that she could trust that he would not pressure her in any way. As he heard Maria apologizing to him, he froze when she mentioned his purity commitment.

Tate reached for her hands; he leaned in and kissed her on the cheek, smiling, because so much joy filling his heart, he asked? "What did you say?"

"I'm sorry."

"No. Not that. "How do you know about my purity commitment?"

"You told me. How else would I know?"

Maria responded and frowned up at him; then, she rubbed her temples.

Tate's heart was racing. *She remembers*, "Yes, I did tell you. Do you remember when?" Seeing his excitement, she knew she remembered something. Trying to recall that information only increased the pain in her temples.

Tate watched her trying to remember; he also saw the level of pain the effort cost. Then, pulling her back into his arms, he said, "Babe, please don't force the memories; they will come. I can't handle seeing you in pain."

"Tate, I want to know, I need to know."

"We can talk about it later after the pain has stopped."

"Will you answer all of my questions?"

"I will, as long as it doesn't cause you any pain. Now, are you ready for your surprise?" Turning her around, she saw her Mustang practically gleaming,

"You detailed my car?" her voice held a bit of wonder in it. "That was on my list for Christmas!" As she walked closer, she couldn't see the dings and dents that she kept promising to fix when she got some extra money. "Tate, she's beautiful! Have you gotten any sleep? I know you do your best work when you can't sleep. Are you okay?"

Smilingly Tate responded, "Although I haven't slept much, lack of sleep wasn't my motivation. Instead, I wanted to impress this beautiful woman and maybe get her thinking about forever with me."

"Well, sir, I've been thinking about forever for days, but Sally's makeover is a definite bonus!" Oh, how she loved this man. Unable to stop herself, Maria grabbed the front of his shirt and pulled him in for a quick hard kiss. "Thank you! Thank you! Thank you! Oh, I got to tell Mama!" Turning, she ran into the house, calling for her mother.

Tate stood in the garage with a massive grin on his face thanking God for Maria and that her memory was coming back. He didn't question how she knew about him restoring cars when he couldn't sleep. Bowing his head, he prayed, *Father, I can't thank You enough for placing Maria in my life. I love her and believe she is the one You have created for me. Father give us the wisdom to keep her safe and to stop Mendez. Show us what to do, Father.*

Tate waited on God; he'd learned from Grams that if you ask God a question, you need to allow Him to respond. So he waited, taking deep breaths and letting them out slowly. He waited. Minutes passed before the thought came to him that he needed to tell Maria about the kidnapping. *She needs to be included in the process; she is stronger than you think.*

Tate wanted to debate that option, he wanted to protect Maria, but he knew God knew best. *Okay, Father, I will tell her after dinner.*

Chapter Sixteen

Maria, so excited about the car, about Tate, about everything, vibrating with joy, found her mom in the kitchen, "Mama! Come see my car. Tate made it look brand new!"

Rosa Rodriguez had watched Maria with Tate. From the moment he rushed into her hospital room and pulled Maria into his arms, she knew that her daughter was in love. "Slow down, sweet girl. What's going on?"

"Mama, I love him! I love Tate Weston." Maria stood in the middle of the kitchen with tears running down her face smiling. "Mama, you were right; love will change you. He's the one for me, Mama."

Rosa walked over to her beautiful daughter, embraced her, and said, "I know, baby, I know. But, this one, he is special; he has won your heart twice."

"Mama, do you and Papa approve? I know you didn't care for Jesse…."

"Oh, baby girl, I know Jesse didn't love you. He didn't treat you badly, but he didn't act like you were special to him."

Maria shook her head as she recalled Jesse's behavior when she decided to stop by his apartment. Her memory was coming back!

Her mom continued, "Now Tate Weston—he is a man in love! He stood up to your father and earned his respect. He has met all of your brothers, and they like him. And he has asked your father if he can court you. This one is serious, and I like him. He loves God, and he loves you, baby girl. So yes, we approve of him."

"Mama, I think it will be a short engagement."

"My baby is in love! The time doesn't matter to me, short or long; when it happens, we will be ready!"

≈≈≈

Dinner was awesome; Maria's whole family showed up. So many conversations were going on. Tate was so happy to be with Maria that it didn't matter who else was in the room. The only cloud over his joy was that he had to tell Maria about Jesse's plans to kidnap her. He prayed that they would have some time to talk after dinner.

Tate helped Maria with the dishes, making small talk until they were finished. As Maria folded the dish towel and put it away, she asked, "So what's on your mind, Tate? You're frowning again."

"I need to tell you what's going on with Jesse." Seeing her interest, he continued, "We did some digging on him and found out that Jesse Mendez is Jesse Ramos. He's Hector and Roberto Ramos' nephew."

Maria listened, wondering why Jesse approached her and why he lied about being engaged to her. Knowing her thoughts, Tate answered her unasked question, "He wanted to get to your father to get information on the scheduled shifts for the best time to move drugs into Peace Valley." Tate shared all the information they had on Jesse, as well as the plan to kidnap her.

"Is that the reason you're here, to keep me safe?"

Seeing her drop her head to hide the hurt in her eyes, Tate moved into her personal space and pulled her into his arms. "Maria, I am here because I love you, and I couldn't stay away. You don't remember, but when I stayed behind to treat Kevin's wound, it was the hardest decision I have ever made. I wanted to be there for you, and I'm sorry I wasn't. I know you are an amazing cop. I've read all about your work here in Peace Valley and the special assignments you've worked on, but right now, you are the woman I love. Everything in me wants to keep you safe, to protect you. I know you can take care of yourself, and you don't need me fighting for you, but do you think I can fight with you?"

Maria listened. Her anger and disappointment vanished the moment he moved into her personal space. Her heart tripped over itself when he said she was an amazing cop; his approval of her was an unexpected gift. All her insides turned to goo when he said she is the woman he loves. And just when she thought she would burst with love for this man, he asked if he could fight with her! Where did this man come from?

So much joy filled her heart that she leaned her head back, and a giggle escaped, then another, and another until she was laughing out loud, holding her side. Tate just watched; after a few minutes, she said, "If you can frown, I can laugh. And for the record, I am so in love with you right now! I don't know...."

Tate cut her words off with an incredible kiss that left them both breathless. When their breathing returned to normal, Maria asked, "So what's the plan? How will we stop Jesse?"

"Your dad and I have a plan; we can talk to him about it."

Nodding her head in agreement, Maria stood on tiptoes, kissed his cheek, and whispered in his ear, "I love you, Dr. Tate Cornelius Weston." Smiling at his surprised expression, she said, I remember.

Grinning, Tate took her hand and said, "I love you too. Maria Roseanna Rodriguez, let's go find your dad."

Chapter Seventeen

Travis took extra care getting dressed for his date; this was a new experience for him. A woman had never picked him up for a date. He had mixed feelings about it. He was thrilled that Susan wanted to treat him, even if it was a bet over a basketball game. He smiled, remembering how he felt making that winning shot. He had to work for every point he made in that game. Susan made him work for it, and that made the win sweet. He could imagine years of them together, winning and losing to each other; at that thought, his smile grew wider on his face. The downside for him, if he could call it that, the downside for him was, he'd never been taken on a date, and he considered it a date. Being the oldest of four brothers, their dad had always taught them to be gentlemen; the man asked the girl out and picked the girl up and paid. Tonight was a total reverse; this was new to him. Although some women had approached him over the years, he had avoided them, thought them forward, too aggressive. With Susan, he was excited about spending time with her and more than a little curious about how this date would go. Hearing the doorbell, he took one quick look at himself in the mirror and headed for the door.

≈≈≈

Driving to Travis' apartment, Susan experienced a merriment of emotions; she had picked up the phone to cancel the date no less than a dozen times. Each time she had hung up, remembering how it felt playing ball with Travis, talking with him, taking selfies with him, and sharing kisses with him. The realistic side of her told her that this budding relationship with Travis would end as soon as he heard the rumors T.J. Muller spread about her; it had happened enough times that she had stopped trying. Yet, the other side of her, that hopeful side, the part of her that caused her to break up with Kevin, that part of her that held out for real love, wouldn't let go of hope. To Susan, Travis Black looked like hope, and as hard as she tried, she couldn't let go of that hope for real love. She had suffered so much, the looks and whispers behind her back, even outright attacks from some. It was a nightmare she didn't want to relive, but the pull of hope was like water to someone dying of thirst; the need couldn't be denied.

Susan decided to talk with Travis, be open and honest about her past, face it, and stop hiding from it. She had learned that if she was honest about how she felt with Kevin, things might have been different, and she and Kevin would still be friends. Susan was determined that the rumors would no longer control her life; it was time to step out of the shadows and take back her life. Pulling to a stop at Travis' apartment, she whispered, "Okay, God, full disclosure. I'll do it, but I need Your help. Give Travis a heart to hear me out. Thank you, Father."

Travis was staring; he couldn't help it. When he opened his door, he wasn't prepared for the beautiful woman standing before him. Susan was amazing, shaking his head; he didn't know how she did it. One moment she was the girl next door playing ball, and the next moment, she was this stunning beauty who would draw the attention of every man in the room. He felt humbled that God would bless him with such a precious gift of her affection. Finding his voice, he greeted, "Hey Susan. You look beautiful." Seeing her blush from his compliment, he grinned and asked, "Where are you taking me? I'm mighty hungry."

Laughing, she said, "The best steakhouse in town." Travis laughed out loud when they pulled up to Mason's Diner. Giving her a questioning eye, she said, "It is the best steakhouse in town, no kidding." Walking in the diner hand in hand, they were escorted to a meeting room in the back of the restaurant. As the hostess opened a small conference room door, he spied a table decked out with fine china, linen table cloths, fresh flowers, and two covered plates.

Travis could hear soft jazz music in the background and smiled; Susan had remembered that he liked jazz. As he noticed how many details she remembered about him and how much effort she put into their dinner, he was so flattered. He felt special, a feeling he had never felt with a woman.

Susan had to keep reminding herself not to get lost looking in Travis' eyes, listening to his voice, or smelling his woodsy scented cologne. Everything about this man drew her. In a handful of days, he had captured her heart so completely that she was reduced to a giggling, phone-toting girl, waiting on his next text or call.

Susan wanted desperately to talk with someone about what happened with Kevin, T.J., and now Travis, but there was no one. As she completed that thought, she remembered a brief encounter with Lilly, Kevin's fiancé, after Sunday service. Susan's upbringing didn't allow her to skip church. She had tried after she found out about the lies T.J. had spread, but after a few weeks, she was miserable. After that, she never missed church; it didn't feel right. She started back but arrived late and left early. That plan had worked to reduce some stress, it took some effort to go, but God was worth it.

Susan had heard that Kevin was seeing someone, and she was glad for him. She wanted to tell him that she was happy for them, but her last conversation with Kevin was when they broke up, and she didn't know how to approach him. So, she prayed that God would allow her to clear things up between them and hopefully mend the friendship they had. That prayer came to mind when Lilly chased her down before she could get to her car. Wow, that petite woman was fast on her feet, even in three-inch heels.

"Susie! Susie!" Lilly weaved through people calling her name.

Chapter Eighteen

Susan turned the corner to the parking lot, moving away from the crowd forming in front of the church, trying her best to ignore her name being called. She wasn't ready to talk to Lilly; she had no idea how that conversation would go. One glance over her shoulder showed her that she wouldn't get away. Slowing her steps and squaring her shoulders, she turned to face Lilly Collins. *God help me.* Removing all expressions from her face, Susan said, "Hello, can I help you?"

Lilly Collins looked up into her eyes with so much compassion that it disarmed Susan. It had felt as if Lilly's brown eyes were looking into her soul and seeing all of her. "Susie, my name is Lilly Collins, and I wanted to let you know how sorry I am about what you are experiencing because of T.J. Muller. I also want to tell you that Kevin doesn't blame you in any way for what T.J. did. Susie, you have more friends than you think, and… I want to be one of them." As Susan stood in shocked surprise, Lilly gave her one of the best hugs she had ever received and whispered, "Just in case you needed one."

Handing her a piece of paper, smiling, Lilly had walked away, saying, "Call me. I would love to talk." Lilly pondered that encounter feeling a smile as she considered Lilly as a friend. She made up her mind that she would give Lilly a call and see.

"Hey, where did you go?" Travis asked, searching her face with curiosity in his voice.

Susan felt like she was at the center of Travis' world. She never imagined how good it felt. Her heart was flooding with emotions.

"Oh, sorry. I was thinking about a girlfriend. I need to give a call."

"Is everything okay?" Before she could answer, they heard a soft tap on the meeting room door before a couple walked in. "Kevin? Kevin, Lilly. Hello, is everything okay?"

"Hi Susie, Travis. Lilly and I are having dinner, and we wanted to know if you wanted to join us, but we see you already have plans. So maybe we can get together next week?" Travis turned to address his soon-to-be boss, "Lt. Weston, please join us."

Kevin looked at Lilly, who gave the slightest shake of her head. Travis would have missed it if he hadn't been trained in observation.

"Thanks for the invite, but it can wait until next week. Susie, Lilly will get with you to see what day works for you. Is that okay?"

Susan addressed Lilly, "Yes, I look forward to speaking with you; in fact, I was hoping to talk with you later tonight or tomorrow if that's possible?"

Lilly responded without hesitation, "Tonight, or tomorrow night, I'm usually up late, so any time before 11:30 p.m. is good."

"Thanks. I'll talk to you later tonight."

Travis could hear the nervousness and hesitation in Susan's voice. He could also see the watchful, protective look Kevin gave him and wondered what was going on. Then it dawned on him. There was some talk around the station about Kevin's girlfriend leaving him for T.J. Muller. Travis felt a sickening feeling in his stomach. Could Susan be like the other women in his life? Would she send him a Dear John text like the others when someone in her mind is a better deal than him? How would he recover from her rejection when he had already practically given her his heart? Did he really know her? Was what he believed they had worth the risk? Travis determined that they needed to talk, and he needed to listen. By the time he lifted his eyes to meet Susan's and realized he was too late, the hurt and resignation he saw in those big beautiful almond-shaped brown eyes cut him to his core. She just stared at him, hurting. *Oh God, I did this to her. Please help me, and please show me what to do.* "Susan, can we talk?"

Susan had watched Travis ponder why Kevin and Lilly wanted to talk with her. At first, it was great timing. She could tell him about Kevin and T.J., but the more he pondered, the more disgusted he looked, the more her hope diminished, the greater became her desire to get away from him. Susan thought he was different, that they had something special, that he could care for her beyond the rumors. She was wrong. Removing all emotions from her voice, standing to push her chair to the table, she said, "No need to talk. Officer Black, thanks for dinner. Goodbye."

Travis went after her, called to her, but once she left the room, she disappeared. Walking home to his car, he felt such admiration for her, the strength she displayed even though he knew she was hurting. He also felt the self-loathing for causing her that pain. Hearing her words echoing in his head, "Goodbye," caused his heart to break, realizing with Susan, he had everything he wanted in a relationship, and in an instant, he had nothing. He prayed, *Father, I know I hurt her, and I know that I love her. Please show me what to do?*

Chapter Nineteen

Susan sat in the tiny unmarked meeting room next to the room she had just exited. She couldn't talk with Travis right now or ever. At least this time, she was the one to walk away.

As hard as she tried, the tears wouldn't stop. All she wanted to do was crawl into her bed, cover her head, and cry for all the dreams she would never have, and she knew that she wouldn't try again. How can you unlove someone once your heart has chosen to love them? And she did love Officer Travis Black. Her buzzing phone had her grabbing for it to silence it before someone, Travis, found her. Swiping to end the call, she missed the off button answering the call and heard Lilly's voice. Looking up to the ceiling, she mouthed, *Really, God!*

"Susie? Susie? Hello?"

"Hi Lilly, I'm here."

"Hey, are you okay?"

"Yeah, just fine."

"He didn't know?"

Susan didn't have the heart or the energy to act like she didn't know who Lilly was talking about. "No, he didn't." She responded flatly.

"Gee Susie, I'm so sorry. We would have waited if we knew you were on a date."

"It's okay; I was planning to tell him about it tonight anyway. So it's no big deal."

There was a long pause, then Lilly responded, "Kevin has to stop by the station, and I need a ride home. Do you mind dropping me off on your way home?"

Rolling her eyes and lifting her gaze to the ceiling again, mouthing, *For real God? Why can't I just go home and cry? Why do I have to do people right now?* Then a thought came to her; *She wants to be your friend, you need her, talk to her, she will hear you.*

"Susie, I can get...."

"No, it's okay. Meet me in my office in five minutes."

Five minutes later, Lilly was in her office, giving her another 'just in case you need a hug,' that opened the floodgates on the tears and loosened her tongue. Susan cried and talked until she was spent, and Lilly listened, laughed, cried, and listened some more. One hour later, sitting quietly at her desk, wondering what she had been thinking, spilling her guts like that.

Lilly began to talk, "So you broke up with Kevin because you didn't feel the marriage kind of love for him?"

"Don't get me wrong. I love Kevin. We've been friends forever, but there were no sparks between us, no attraction. Do you know what I mean?"

Blushing, Lilly said, "No, I don't know what you mean."

Susan responded with a grin, "Does he curl your toes?"

Lilly grinned back, "Girl, I'm afraid to wear open-toe sandals."

They both fell out in a fit of giggles, and for the first time in a very long time, Susan claimed someone as a friend.

Lifting her eyes to the ceiling for the third time that night, she mouthed, *Thank You, God. You were right. I needed her.* Then they talked about the men in their lives, how they met and fell in love.

Susan could hardly believe she was talking about their boyfriends like best friends. Then she remembered that Travis wasn't her boyfriend, and after tonight he never would be, and the pain in her heart caused her to tear up again.

"Susie, do you love Travis?"

Wiping tears, Susan responded without hesitation, "I feel like I have waited my whole life for him. So yes, I love him."

"Then you're going to have to talk to him; find out what happened tonight. Tell him your side of the story, not the rumors, and trust God with the outcome."

With a fresh wave of tears, Susan said, "Lilly, I don't know if I can take it if he walks away from me."

"Then write him a letter, send him a text, let him know that there is more than the rumors. Give him something to hold on to Susie, and try to remember that he has a story too."

"Okay, when I get home, I'll text him."

Lilly smiled, stood up, and said, "Alrighty, let's go. If we hurry, you can drop me off and be home before ten o'clock. Oh, by the way, what are you doing on Saturday? I am going shopping for some closed-toe sandals. Want to come with me?"

"Sure, I'm free; maybe by then, I'll need a pair too." Then, laughing, they left the diner.

Chapter Twenty

Travis was beyond frustrated. He'd called Susan; she hadn't responded. He hated the silence, hated not knowing if she was okay, hated himself for hurting her, and hated the thought of not having her in his life.

When he got home, he got his truck and drove by her house; she wasn't there. He then drove back to the diner; she wasn't there. With each disappointment, the tiny thread of hope he held that she would forgive him and give him another chance slipped away.

Travis didn't want to go home; going home felt like giving up, and he wasn't willing to let Susan go. Driving around town, he saw the park he and Susan played basketball and was drawn to it.

Parking in the lot and grabbing his basketball from the back of his SUV, he walked on the court, dribbling, shooting, and remembering the time he'd spent with Susan.

Hearing a car pull up and park brought Travis from his thoughts of Susan. Travis stood alert, wondering who or what trouble would be out here at this hour. Assessing his vulnerability, his shoulders relaxed when he saw Kevin Weston.

"Hi, Travis."

"Hi, Kevin. What are you doing out here?"

Kevin walked to a bench at the edge of the court and sat down, "I saw your truck in the parking lot and wanted to talk with you. And since my fiancé is with your girlfriend right now, I figured we needed to talk before the rumors get to you."

Travis sat next to Kevin, let out a frustrated breath, and said, "Too late for that."

"What do you mean?"

"I mean, I figured it out while we were together, now Susan won't talk with me. I told her we needed to talk, but she read my expressions all wrong, told me there was no need to talk, and left."

"What happened? What did you say."

"I didn't say anything, but when it dawned on me that all the talk around the station when I first got here was about you, her, and T.J., I wondered if she was like the other women I dated who would dump me when a better choice came along. By the time I realize that we needed to talk about it, she had misread my expressions. I know I hurt her, and I didn't mean to. I don't know what happened. What I heard wasn't good, but I would have listened to her, Kevin."

"Well, I know you need to talk with Susie, but I'd like to share my side of what happened with our relationship." Kevin paused as if collecting his thoughts before saying, "Susie didn't break up with me to date T.J. Muller. She broke up with me because we didn't love each other. Back then, I didn't want to accept that, and T.J. played it up as if she wanted him just to mess with my head. That man hated that I made rank before he did. Susie was his way to get back at me.

I was angry with Susie for a long while until I started courting Lilly. What I have with Lilly is worlds away from what Susie and I had. Lilly and I had talked about it and agreed that we wanted to clear the air between us. That's why we stopped by the diner tonight.

Susie did me a favor by ending our relationship, but it cost her dearly. T.J. spread so many lies about her that the people who didn't know her and some who just like to gossip blew this out of proportion. People can be cruel.

Susie had stopped dating some time ago; that's why I was surprised to see you two together. I'm not sure how bad you've messed up, but from what I saw tonight, she cares for you."

"How do you know that she cares?"

"The way she looked at you tonight and the fact that she cooked for you," Travis looked puzzled.

Kevin went on, "You had steak tonight, right?"

"Yes."

"The only way you can get a steak in that restaurant is that she cooks it. Steak is not on the menu, my friend, and to my knowledge, it never has been."

"Has she ever made you a steak?" Kevin was quiet for a few seconds too long, agitating Travis to no end. "No, she never made me a steak, and she never arranged a private dinner for me. Travis, she cares. Give her a little time. She's talking with Lilly right now. When she's ready, she'll talk. Be ready to listen."

A huge smile spread across Travis' face as hope welled up inside of him. Travis left the park, thanking God for the hope of another chance with Susan and praying it wouldn't take too long before he could see her again.

Arriving home, Travis decided to take a shower and get ready for work. He had an early shift, so he followed his nightly routine of preparing for the next day before getting into a hot shower. Walking out of the bathroom while towel drying his hair, he heard his phone indicating a text. Tossing the towel down, he grabbed his phone. Seeing Susan's name started his heart pounding. Opening the text,

Susan: "Hi."

Travis whispered a thank you to God and asked for wisdom, not to mess up again.

Travis: "Hi. How are you?"
Susan: "Better. Can we talk?"
Travis: "Yes! Just tell me where and when."
Susan: "The park, in 10 minutes."
Travis: "I'll be there! Thank you, Susan."

Chapter Twenty-One

Susie watched Travis get out of his truck after parking beside her car. He looked like he had just gotten out of the shower, hair still wet, wearing a black tee-shirt and black sweatpants. Seeing him again, her heartbeat accelerated. She realized again that she had been waiting for this man her whole life. Praying once more, *Father, give him a listening ear and an understanding heart.* She got out of her car, walked to the bench, and waited for him.

Travis' eyes drank in Susan; he was amazed at how beautiful she looked in her pink sweatsuit with matching sneakers. She was simply the most beautiful woman he had ever known inside and out.

He'd kicked himself over and over for thinking she was like the other women he had dated, even for a second. He knew that she was different and would do whatever it took to make things right between them. Taking a deep breath and rubbing his sweaty palms on his pant legs, he spoke, "Hi Susan. Thank you for meeting with me.'

"Thank you for coming." Susan scooted over so Travis could sit next to her on the bench. A few minutes passed before she started talking once he settled on the bench giving her his full attention.

"Kevin and I were friends all through school; we never dated, although we always ended up at the same events. I have always loved Kevin as a friend, so it wasn't a big deal when he asked me to be his plus one for a couple of events. If I could describe our relationship, I would say it was comfortable.

Over time we became a couple. When Sidney and J.P. announced their engagement, I noticed that their relationship was very different from ours. Their love was so strong it felt tangible. It was so beautiful. They had what I wanted, real love, heart-stopping, toe-curling love, real love. I didn't have that with Kevin.

I realized to continue in a relationship with Kevin, I would be settling, and so would he. Even though we liked each other, we didn't love each other, not the marrying kind of love. Once I realized that I started pulling back. I began dropping hints to Kevin, but he was so caught up in his job, he didn't get it.

The day Kevin saw me with T.J. Muller was so random. It was the first time I had talked with T.J. He just sat at my table, introduced himself, and started talking. A few minutes later, Kevin walked in. He assumed that I was cheating on him. I should have told him what happened, but I was mad at him for believing the worst of me, and I knew it was time to end our relationship.

I told him that he loved his job more than me. It was the coward's way out, but I didn't know that T.J. had planned our meeting to get back at Kevin. I meet with T.J. one other time where he apologized, said he was so sorry, and offered his friendship. When we departed, he hugged me. I found out later that he had someone taking pictures of us.

By the time I found out about it, T.J. had spread so many lies around town, my reputation was shot. So I didn't break up with Kevin to be with T.J. I broke up with Kevin because I didn't love him, and he didn't love me.

Travis listened; his hope grew as she spoke. His heart went out to her when she talked about how she was treated when the rumors started. Travis reached out and held her hand, offering comfort and encouragement, needing to touch her, needing to connect with her. Susan turned those gorgeous almond-shaped brown eyes on him, and he couldn't speak, couldn't think. He realized that Susan was his future, and God was giving him the privilege to look into those eyes for the rest of his life. Travis was awestruck.

"If I had known then what T.J. Muller was planning, I would have told Kevin everything. I didn't mean to hurt him; I just wanted real love." Falling silent, Susan waited.

Travis, still holding Susan's hand, understanding what happened with Kevin and T.J., that she didn't have any romantic feelings for either of them, encouraged him to share his heart. He questioned himself, how could he not share? Susan had shared all, and he felt like he knew all of her, a feeling he had never experienced with anyone else, and for the first time, he wanted someone to know all of him; no, not someone, he wanted Susan to know all of him. Lifting her hand to his lips, he kissed it and took a deep breath inhaling her scent; he began.

"I need to make some things clear to you; his voice was low, causing her to lean closer to hear him. When I saw Kevin and Lilly, I remembered some talk around the station about Kevin's girlfriend breaking up with him for T.J. Susan, the same thing that happened to me a few times.

Each time, it seems like they were only with me until something better came along. I didn't know that the talk was about you. So, when I realized it was you, I had so many questions and thoughts going through my mind, but I wanted to talk, I wanted to hear your story. I would have listened, Susan." Seeing her gentle smile, he continued, "I started falling for you at the restaurant when you walked up to me and called me "Babe." I thought I was dreaming. I didn't even know your name, but it felt right, and when you told me what was happening, I was amazed at how brave you were."

Travis paused to collect his thoughts, he didn't want to ramble, but he wanted her to know how he felt about her. Glancing up to her, he saw she was listening, waiting, giving him time to process before speaking. He added something else to the ever-growing list of qualities he loved about Susan Mason.

Susan listened to Travis, awed by him and God. Never in her wildest dreams could she have imagined anyone saying the wonderful things he was sharing with her about her! Who is this beautiful, amazing, intelligent, courageous woman he was talking about? She almost looked over her shoulder to see if that woman was standing behind her. Travis cradled her chin in his hand as if he was reading her mind; he said, "Susan, that's how I see you; that's who I'm falling in love with."

Her scarred, battered heart was beating with hope in her chest from his words pouring healing balm over her heart. He loves me! He loves me! She repeated it over and over in her head, causing a huge smile to appear on her face.

Travis cupped her face with both hands, mesmerized by her, drawing her to a standing position. He pulled her close, gathering her in his arms, looking into her eyes, vulnerable and confident at the same time. Then, lowering his head, he kissed her, taking his time to enjoy every sensation, every sigh she gave him.

When he pulled back and looked at her again, her eyes were closed; she looked as if she was savoring their moment. Oh, how he loved this woman! Pulling her close, holding her in the quiet night, Travis thanked God for Susan Mason and promised to treasure her all the days of his life.

The sound of squeaking breaks interrupted the quiet night. Immediately Travis' senses were on the alert; something big was coming their way. Seeing trucks' headlights getting closer, he pulled Susan away from the bench into hedges.

Something wasn't right, very few work trucks moved through Resting Place after regular business hours, and it was almost midnight.

Travis reached in his pocket for his phone and dialed Ben Rayns. As he Peeked over the bench, he reported seeing three big dump trucks heading toward the interstate.

After hanging up, he turned to Susan, gathered her close, and kissed her again before saying in a husky voice, "Susan, I'm going to follow you home, then I have to go to work. I think the shipment has come in early." Seeing the concern on her face, he kissed her again.

"Travis, please be careful." She whispered, "I can't lose you now that…."

Travis lifted her chin and looked into her beautiful brown eyes, and said, "Susan, I love you too, and I promise to be careful. Now let's get you home."

Chapter Twenty-Two

No! No way! I don't like it. Tate's emotions went from simple irritation to outright anger. He continued staring down every man at the table, including Chief Rodriguez, before continuing, "There is no way on God's green earth that I'm going to let Mendez take her anywhere. He couldn't believe what they were asking. *Breathe Tate, he reminded himself.*

He knew something was up, and their plans had to be adjusted when he got word that Travis had sighted three dump trucks a couple of hours ago. He knew they had to act fast, and he also knew that they had nothing. They were flying blind.

Ben had suggested they play dumb and let Mendez lead them to the drugs by allowing them to take Maria. She would have a tracker and lead them right to Mendez and, hopefully, the drugs.

He knew it was the only plan that made sense, but he didn't like Maria being the bait; that thought twisted his gut. How could they? Look what happened the last time. What if something went wrong? What if he lost her again? "She's still recovering." No one said a word. Tate was about to speak again when he felt Maria take his hand. "Tate, can we take a walk?"

Without saying a word, they walked out of the house. Once outside, she pulled him close, saying, "Tate, it's my job?"

"I know, I know, and I know you need to do this. But it just makes me crazy to think Mendez taking you or hurting you. I love you so much; I don't want you hurt again."

Maria looked into Tate's eyes, seeing the love he has for her. Her heart melted for this man all over again. She felt incredibly blessed to have him in her life and couldn't wait for them to start their life together. But tonight, she needed to do her job and trust God to keep her in the process. "Tate, my dad, and Ben have taken every precaution to keep me safe. I'm even wearing a tracker right now with a wire, so not only can you see where I am, but you can also hear where I am. Tate, it's my job…." Maria stopped talking, not knowing what else she could say. In the past, if anyone had dared question her about her job or tried to treat her any differently from her male counterparts, she would have given them an earful, then proved them wrong. She knew her job; her training was by the best, her dad and her brothers. She was often called in for high-level assignments because of her skillset. At this moment, none of that mattered to her; she wanted, needed Tate's okay.

Tate listened to Maria while at the same time, listened to the sounds of the night. Uncle Ben had taught them how to filter nature's sounds on many of their camping trips to identify what belongs and what doesn't. Warning bells were sounding in his head. Someone was watching them. He recognized the silence as every creature paused to listen, then he heard the faint rustling of leaves in the woods.

They had come for her, and with God's help, he would let them take her. Pulling her even closer, he whispered in her ear, "Maria, I get it and won't try to stop you. I love you, and I am trusting God to keep you safe." Then, lowering his voice, he said, "Listen, stay alert; they're here." Lifting her hand, he kissed her wrist and spoke into her watch, "Ben, two men behind me."

Maria's adrenaline spiked as she watched Tate relay a message to Ben Rayns. It was happening; they had come for her. She was ready, feeling Tate relax his body before hearing a thud and seeing him fall to the ground. Stepping back in a fighting stance, everything in her screamed that her partner was down, and she should have his back. Maria knew that she could handle the two men attacking them; she'd trained to fight two to three opponents at once. Knowing she had to be taken, she determined that the guy who hit Tate would also suffer a blow before she gave up the fight. Releasing a forced scream, she balled up her fist and delivered a punch to his nose and was rewarded with his cry of pain, then mumbling something about a broken nose before being grabbed from behind with a gun pressed hard into her back. Resisting the urge to fight back, she allowed them to drag her away.

Tate watched as the two men dragged Maria away. He was assured of her skills as he watched her land a fist to one of the men's noses and broke it. She could fight, but it didn't remove the crunch in his gut at the thought of Mendez being near her. Once they were out of sight and he could no longer hear them in the woods, he got up, rubbing the back of his head, and ran to the house.

"Uncle Ben, do you have her?" Tate asked breathlessly as he ran into the house.

"Yes! We have her. We can hear them talking; they're taking her over to Valley View, which's a residential area. Tony has already sent three patrol cars over there. Let's make it too hot there for them to stay, and hopefully, they will lead us to Mendez."

"Look! Cops, we can't stay here." A frustrated, angry voice came across the speaker. "Call the Boss!" Then, hearing the ringing of a phone, they waited; after the fourth ring, Tate and Tony's eyes met as they recognized Jesse's voice.

"Do you have my package?"

"Yeah, we have her now, we are at the location, but there are cops all over the place. We can't risk getting caught, leaving her here. What now? Do you want us to take care of this?"

"No! Bring her here!"

"Mr. Hunter said that no one but us should know about the drop point." Tate could hear Jesse's anger at being questioned.

"Do you work for Hunter now?"

"No, Boss! It's just…." Tate could hear the fear in the man's voice."

"No, Boss, I work for you. We'll bring her to the warehouse."

≈≈≈

Jesse hit the end button for the call, livid that his man questioned his decision. Enraged that Stevenson had talked with his men without him, going behind his back, making his men doubt him. Stevenson was up to something, he knew it, and he knew it would end tonight. Jesse determined in his heart that Hunter Stevenson would pay for messing with Jesse Ramos. He needed to gain control of his people, and he needed to send a strong message. Jesse reached for his phone, dialed, then spoke, "I need a favor."

A digital voice came over the phone, "My favors are not cheap, are you willing to pay my price?"

"More than willing, I have a number. I want the owner of this number eliminated tonight. Can you do it?"

"One million, I will wire you an account. You have fifteen minutes to pay the fee. Once the fee is received, your request will be located and eliminated. Your confirmation will be a text from the owner's phone stating the requested job has been completed. Do we have a deal?"

"Yes." The call ended with a soft click followed by a chime indicating the arrival of a text. Smiling, Jesse moved to an old metal desk in the corner of the room. Ten minutes later, Jesse released a breath as he made the one-million-dollar transfer, labeled as a donation, grinning as he imagined Hunter Stevenson eliminated. Leaning back in his chair, he laughed out loud, enjoying this victory. Hearing the sound of a car approaching, he whispered, "Welcome, my little Ice Princess, it's time for your meltdown."

Chapter Twenty-Three

Hunter sat in his car, grinning like a fool. His plans to get rid of Jesse were working out better than he could have imagined. Jesse, that stupid, foolish man, just paid him one million dollars and signed his own death warrant. Hunter almost laughed out loud when Jesse called the burner phone; he set up for targeted assignments. Hunter had given the number to Roberto to gain favor over a year ago. Roberto has used the service a couple of times, giving Hunter access and favor with the Drug Lord. Jesse must have gotten it from Roberto. It didn't matter now how he got the phone number. It was a gift, and Hunter wouldn't look this gift horse in the mouth. Smiling, he then sent a text to his point man and entered Jesse's cell number for an assigned hit for tonight. Yes, sir, service with a smile. Twenty minutes later, after driving to the peer on the backside of the loading docks, he texted Jesse's phone, *Your requested assignment has been finalized. Thank you for your donation!*

After sending the text, Hunter removed the SIM card, got out of his car, walked to the end of the peer, and tossed the phone in the water.

Feeling great satisfaction, he checked his watch; his plane would leave in the next hour, just enough time to reach Roberto Ramos' New York home before word got to him that his nephew's delivery went sour and Jessie died in the process. His plan was foolproof! Laughing at his humor, he headed for Baltimore-Washington International Airport.

At the first stoplight, he reached into the glove box, pulled out a new burner phone, and dialed Peace Valley Police Department with an anonymous tip. Hunter was already making mental notes on how he would take over the 'Jesse project as the light turned green.'

≈≈≈

Tate watched the little car on the GPS tracking system on the computer, praying for Maria, praying that God would keep him calm because he felt like he was about to come unglued. Sitting around doing nothing when the woman he loved was in danger was not working for him. He needed to do something, and all the pent-up energy desperately needed an outlet. Standing, he started pacing, praying with every step that this night would end well. *Father, I trust You and know that You love Maria far more than I do. Please keep her safe tonight.*

Hearing the phone ring, Tate headed back to the kitchen. Recognizing Sam Alexander's voice, he turned a questioning glance to Uncle Ben. "I asked Sam to check out any possible locations they could be used for storage." Ben answered his unasked question before addressing Sam, "Hey Sam, what have you found?"

"I'm near the old abandoned warehouse on Freight Street across from the Waste and Recycle Center. There is a lot of activity for an empty building. I'm going to get a closer look. I'll let you know if I find anything."

"Great work, Sam! According to Maria's tracker, she's heading your way."

Tony added, "I'll get some units over there ASAP!" as the call ended, Travis hurriedly gathered the laptop while the others headed for their vehicles. Tate headed for the garage when Tony said, "I'll ride with you."

"Okay." Turning to respond, Tate saw Tony embrace Rosa, whispering in her ear and giving her a parting kiss that said more than words. Tate experienced an instant longing to hold Maria and tell her how much he loved her. Turning away, he prayed, *I trust You, Father. Please keep Maria safe.*

≈≈≈

Maria balled in a fetal position in the trunk of an old burgundy Buick Impala, trying to breathe through the dirty sack placed over her head. Feeling the car come to a stop, she angled her head over her right shoulder and said, "Okay, you guys, I am going to try to stall Jesse until you get here, so be quick about it." Smiling when she heard her brother, LT, 'Little Tony's response, "We're coming, Ms. Bossy." Being the oldest, she had been called that all her life. She had earned the title and was proud of it. Her brothers respected her, and it felt good knowing they knew she could handle herself. She would make them proud tonight. "Well, come on, slowpoke." Her smile disappeared when the trunk was opened, and she was roughly pulled from the car trunk. She was guessing the guy with the broken nose did that as payback. No matter if she had the chance, she would hit him again. Performing a quick assessment of her condition, she determined that she could fight the two guys with a reasonable probability of success, but she couldn't fight three men, especially if one of those men were Jesse. She could beat him if it were just him, but Jesse didn't fight fair; she would need all her wits, no distractions. Her best weapon, for now, was to face off with Jesse and get him talking, play on his ego, challenge him, narrow the playing field to just the two of them.

"Bring her over here." Maria could hear the triumph in his voice as she was shoved from behind. She adjusted her eyes to the dim pole light before looking into Jesse's grinning face. Did he really think this was going to be easy, that she wouldn't fight him? Oh, he wanted her to fight; his ego won't let him believe he would lose to her. Maria prayed, *Father, give me this victory. Give me the words and give me the strength to fight in Jesus' name.* Peace poured over Maria, and she knew without a doubt that she would be okay. Staring Jesse down, Maria smiled and said, "Oh, it's you. I should have known you couldn't handle the job yourself." Maria heard Jesse's quick intake of breath and knew she had made her mark. Taking advantage of his surprise, look at her words. She had always considered her words when talking to anyone, especially Jesse, when explaining her need to avoid physical contact in their relationship. But, today, she would throw caution to the wind in hopes of buying time and finding an opportunity to escape.

The cold stare in Jesse's eyes made her straighten her spine. He would kill her tonight. She knew it. Jesse wanted her to see it, maybe to scare her. Maria still felt the peace she received after praying, so she would continue to push every button Jesse had until he made a mistake. "Coward!" She shouted. Seeing his fist aimed at her face, she ducked under his arm with the grace of a dancer. "Oh, you going to hit me while I'm tied up. Coward!"

Chapter Twenty-Four

Tate continued his constant prayer for Maria's safety and accelerated, pushing his Oldsmobile 442 to its limits to get to Maria.

Tate listened, shocked. *What is she doing? This guy is crazy. Father, please keep her safe.* Turning his attention to Tony, who appeared to be cool, calm, and collected. He asked, "Tony, what is she doing?"

"Tate, she knows what she is doing. She's stalling — playing on Jesse's emotions, buying us time to get to her. And if I know my daughter, she's ready for a fight. As long as we can hear her, she's okay."

≈≈≈

Jesse saw red! Who was this woman? The Little Ice Princess was a she-devil. Coward! Never had he been called a coward! He wanted to shut her up, a fist to the face would have done the trick, but no, she had to duck under his arm and continued calling him a coward, accusing him of beating on a defenseless woman. Well she will see who's the coward, and he would make her bow down to him. She would beg him for mercy. Yes, she would beg, and there would be no mercy. "Untie her!" Jesse shouted.

Once Maria's hands were loosed, the fight was on. She charged Jesse, throwing punches, landing several blows to his head before he could shove her back, knocking her to the ground. Hearing his phone ring, she advanced again, determined to keep him busy until help arrived. She saw Jesse toss his phone to the man with the broken nose. Heard him answer it and say, "What donation? We didn't make no donation." Then saw him fall to the ground dead, blood oozing from his head. With fear in his eyes, she saw Jesse turn, run to his car, and drive away. The other man took off after Jesse left.

Speaking into her watch, she said, "I don't know what just happened, but I got one dead man, and the other two ran away, maybe heading in your direction." Maria heard Travis Black respond, "I see some headlights coming my way. I got this one."

≈≈≈

Jesse drove slowly down the narrow back road with his headlights off. He had done his homework and checked out every warehouse in Peace Valley to ensure an escape route was planned. Uncle Roberto had taught him well.

He'd driven the path before and knew it would take him to the edge of town where he had another car waiting with money and his uncle's jet on standby. If he hurried, he could be in New York in time to explain to Uncle Roberto what happened. Hitting the steering wheel several times to work off some anger, this was not how tonight was supposed to end. Jesse knew his answer wasn't in the anger. As he drove in the dark, he went over every detail of the last few days. His plan was sound. Even Uncle Roberto had agreed.

Something was niggling at the edge of his mind. What was it? Then it came to him. The donation! He had been set up, and he had a sinking feeling that he knew who did it.

≈≈≈

Tate rushed into the warehouse, pausing to scan the room for her, "Maria, where are you?" Seeing her step from behind the opened door. He pulled her into a bone-crushing hug, whispering his thanks to God and his love for her. Maria sighed, pulling back slightly to look into Tate's eyes. The love she saw there made everything disappear as he lowered his lips to hers.

Tate was amazed that oxygen was not high on the list of essentials for living because, at this moment, Maria topped the list, and oxygen was a distant second, as their kiss deepened. God, how he loved this woman, and he couldn't let her go.

"Tate, we still have work to do here." Tony Rodriguez said with some humor in his voice.

Pulling away from Tate, Maria ran to her dad, who scooped her up into another bone-crushing hug, then L.T. hugged her joking about why she let the guy run away. Then patting her on the head told her she'd done an excellent job.

Police were everywhere; she saw her fellow officers, now and then, one would approach her and congratulate her on the drug case. She didn't feel worthy of the praise; a lot of people were involved on so many levels. She had heard about Susan Mason, who told Officer Travis Black about the kidnapping plans. She said to her Dad that Susan Mason had to be recognized for her bravery.

As they cleaned up the crime scene, Tate stuck by her side as they worked side by side. She found that she liked it, liked that he let her do her job and didn't try to pamper her. Ben Rayns had mentioned working with the Response Team, and the thought of working with Tate was appealing. She was feeling blessed.

"What are you smiling about?" Tate eased up behind her, pulling her into his arms.

"The future."

Smiling, Tate asked, "The near future." Turning to face him, Maria responded, "Yes, the very near future."

≈≈≈

On his way home, Travis called Susan. He just wanted to hear her voice. His cell ranged once before she answered, "Hey, you okay?"

"Yes, I'm heading home, but I wanted to hear your voice and see if you want to go out with me tomorrow night?"

"Yes, I would love to go out with you."

"Great, I'll pick you up a 7:30 p.m., goodnight Susan. I love you."

"Goodnight Travis, I love you too."

≈≈≈

Jesse unlocked Uncle Roberto's front door in New York. Unfortunately, he didn't have a phone and didn't know who he could trust to call at this point. So when Jesse walked into the kitchen for something cold to drink before looking for Uncle Roberto, he was shocked to see Hunter Stevenson sitting at the kitchen table with his uncle.

Roberto sprang to his feet and grabbed Jesse into a bear hug. "Nephew, you are well? I thought I had lost you." The joy he saw in his Uncle's eyes warmed him.

"Yes, Uncle. I am well. The delivery was late, one of my men was shot in the head, and then the police came. I had an escape route already planned out, just like you taught me, Uncle." Jesse never took his eyes off Hunter. The shocked look he tried to hide told the story.

Roberto Ramos loosened his grip and sighed. "It is a good thing Hunter delayed sending the full shipment. We are finished with that small town. Jesse, we have to get you out of the States as soon as possible." Reaching for his phone, he said, "You leave tonight. I am sending you to Your cousin Vincent, prepare yourself, you will leave within the hour.

Jesse turned to leave the room, then turned back. "Uncle, somebody tipped the police off. I plan to find out who and how they did it, and I will deal with them."

Smiling, Roberto responded, "You and all of the Ramos family will deal with them. We will deal with traitors, it's personal, and we will take care of them." Smiling at Hunter, Jesse walked out of the room.

≈≈≈

Hunter watched Jesse and Roberto. The affection he saw between them was unexpected. The family loyalty they shared caused his blood to run cold. Jesse suspected him, but he wasn't sure. He realized he might have underestimated Jesse and that it would be to his advantage to put some distance between him and the Ramos family.

Epilogue

Six months later, Maria sat on her bed, looking around her bedroom. After today she would be Mrs. Tate Cornelius Weston. Over the last six months, her life had changed entirely. Her small circle of friends had expanded to include her soon-to-be sisters-in-law. Those amazing women have proven to be friends in all kinds of weather. Getting to know them had been easy. They called, they stopped by, they invited her to every event and even included her brothers, especially when playing basketball, which was at least once a week. She and Tate also spent time with her new best friend, Susan Mason, and her fiancé Travis Black, who also participated in the basketball games. Maria was glad she had grown up with her three brothers because those Weston women could really play basketball. Smiling to herself, because after tonight, she would be one of those Weston Women.

Maria was also included in Kevin and Lilly's small intimate wedding. They made her feel like family, and she loved every one of them, especially Grams, who gave the most amazing hugs. She could hardly believe the love she and

Tate shared and was so happy to be joining his family. Tate had spent time with her Dad and brothers. Last week all the men had gone on a camping trip with Ben Rayns and her Dad. They seemed to have had a great time and were planning another trip in the next few months.

Tate Weston had courted her! Just thinking about that man made her heart speed up and her stomach do somersaults. He treated her as if she was the finest of treasures. Of course, they didn't always agree, but she knew his heart, that he loved her and always wanted the best for her. That one bit of knowledge made their discussions productive, and they found out that compromise was the best segway to making up, and they enjoyed making up.

Hearing a knock at her door, she called, "Come in."

Rosa Rodriquez walked into the room with a huge smile on her face. "Good morning, Baby Girl. How are you feeling? Are you ready to become Mrs. Weston?"

"Mama, I am so ready. I can't believe how blessed I am to be marrying Tate."

"Sweet girl, your Dad and I are so happy for you and Tate. He is a good man, and he loves my Maria! We are so delighted." Pulling a long narrow box out of the pocket of her housecoat, she handed it to Maria. "My mother gave me these pearls on my wedding day to your father. I want you to have them today."

Maria recognized the beautiful pearl necklace; her mother only wore it on special occasions. "Oh, Mama, they are so beautiful! I will take good care of them and pass them on to my daughter."

After putting the pearls around Maria's neck, Rosa hugged her daughter close and said, "I hear your new sisters have arrived to help you get dress. Your father and I will be heading for the church in a few minutes. I love you, Maria."

"I love you too, Mama."

≈≈≈

Tate Weston stood with his brothers Kevin, Marcus, and his brother-in-law J.P. at the alter, waiting for the ceremony to begin. Kevin leaned near and asked, "Nervous?"

Tate took a deep breath and responded, "Yes, but in a good way. I love Maria, and I can't wait for her to be my wife. But I also want to do it right. Uncle Ben has always told us about Dad and Mom and how much they loved each other, and I want that for Maria and me. I want our children to grow up knowing what that looks like." Kevin smiled and said, "Me too, little brother. I want that for Lilly and me too."

As the music changed to the wedding march, Tate couldn't take his eyes off Maria as she and her father walked to the alter. She was simply the most beautiful woman he had ever known. When they reached the alter, Tony hugged Tate and said, "Rosa and I love you, Tate, and we trust you to take care of our little girl." Their love and trust almost brought tears to Tate's eyes. Unable to talk past the emotions Tony's words caused, Tate nodded. Taking Maria's hands, for the first time, he looked in those honey-brown eyes and saw forever. He sent a silent prayer of thanksgiving to God for Maria.

Pastor Mike began talking. Maria listened, amazed that it only took one day to find the love of her life.

"Tate and Maria have chosen their own vows. Tate…"

Tate took both of Maria's hands, looked deeply into her eyes, and began. "Maria, before I met you, I didn't believe in love at first sight. But when we first met, when I shook your hand and looked into your eyes, my whole world shifted. Within hours of meeting you, we were sharing our hopes, dreams, and secrets. I fell in love with you that day. I am so grateful to God and your parents for the opportunity to love you for the rest of my life. Today, before God and man, I pledge to you, my heart. I promise to love, honor, and cherish you. With God's help, I promise to support you in becoming the woman God has created you to be. I promise to lead you, follow you and walk beside you into our destiny, into our forever. Today I commit myself to you, my love, loyalty, fidelity, all that I am and ever hope to be, I give to you."

Maria listened with tears flowing down her cheeks. Tate moved closer and wiped them away, whispering his love for her. Maria was overwhelmed with love for this man as she stared at him with wonder and love remembering their first day together and all the events that brought them to this amazing day. Pastor Mike's voice drew her back.

"Maria…"

"Tate, I didn't believe in love at first sight either, but I'm here today because I fell in love with you twice. The first time was truly love at first sight, and after a few hours in your company, everyone and everything I held dear shifted to give you first place in my life. All of a sudden, my forever had a face and a name. Then I lost my memory. When told I had lost some of my short-term memory. I told myself it was no big deal; it was just a couple of days, nothing major, until you walked into my hospital room and pulled me into your arms. That day, I felt something I have never felt with any man outside of my father and brothers. I felt safe. Then all I wanted was to know what happen that weekend, what we were to each other. I didn't understand then why you kept coming to see me or how your voice was so familiar to me, but I thank God you never gave up on me, on us." Wiping more tears, she took a deep breath and continued. "You kept showing up when I needed you. You were so kind, caring, sweet, considerate, and I kept falling more in love with you. I finally realized I didn't need to remember if we were in love before because I was in love now, and I stopped thinking about what I'd lost and realized what I had. Tate Weston, I love you with all my heart, and I pledge to you today before God and man my heart. I promise to love, honor, and respect you. I promise, with God's help, to encourage you to strive to be the man God has created you to be. I promise to always believe in us, pray for us and fight for us. Today I commit myself to you, my love, trust, loyalty, fidelity, all that I am and ever hope to be, I give to you. Tate you are my hero, and I am honored to be your wife and walk with you into our forever."

Pastor Mike drew Maria and Tate's eyes back to him as he prayed over their rings and led them in the ring exchange. When he pronounced them as husband and wife and told Tate he could salute his wife. The rest of the world disappeared as their eyes met and locked. Grinning, Tate said, "Well, Mrs. Weston, are you ready to begin our forever?"

Maria, smiling back, "Yes, Dr. Weston, I am ready."

Tate lowered his head and claimed his wife's lips and realized that now he didn't mind when she called him Dr. Weston.

The End

THANK YOU!

Thank you for reading Resting Place Déjà Vu. If you enjoyed this book, please, consider recommending it to friends.

Please also consider telling others why you liked this book by leaving a review on the retail site you purchased it.

COMING SOON!

If you want to find out what happens with Trace and Maggie, check out, Resting Place Guardians – Cowboy, book one in the Guardians Series.

OTHER BOOKS BY MARY BEASLEY

Resting Place ~ Phoenix
Can love last a lifetime? Sidney Weston asked this question repeatedly as she tried desperately for ten years to fall out of love with J.P. Carter, her childhood friend and first love. Sidney was forced to leave behind everyone and everything she loved because she dared to cross cultural lines in a relationship with J.P. Carter

She was told she wasn't good enough. She moved to New York and was successful at a major IT company until she dared to pursue a senior executive position. She was then told that she was not a good fit, not good enough. Trusting God, she returned to Resting Place for a new start, only to discover her feelings for J.P. hadn't diminished, even though he had moved on with his life. Will Sidney trust God to find the answer in Resting Place.

Resting Place ~ Safe Haven
Lillian Collin is haunted by a recurring nightmare she can't forget. She's lost everything but is determined to have justice for her brother's death. Hidden away in a safe house with a bounty on her head, Lilian is the only witness who can destroy a drug cartel.

Officer Kevin Weston is haunted by a nightmare he can't remember. Try as he might, he can't recall what happened the night his parents died. Kevin is assigned to protect Lillian while in the witness protection program. As their feelings grow and danger draws near, can they trust God to lead them to their safe haven?

For the latest news on new releases and book sales, visit www.lminow.com

Made in the USA
Middletown, DE
08 October 2022